Raised as a Goon

Ghost

Lock Down Publications and Ca$h Presents

Raised as a Goon

A Novel by *Ghost*

Lock Down Publications

P.O. Box 1482
Pine Lake, Ga 30072-1482

First Edition September 2017
Printed in the United States of America

Lock Down Publications
Like our page on Facebook: Lock Down Publications @
www.facebook.com/lockdownpublications.ldp
Cover design and layout by: **Dynasty Cover Me**
Book interior design by: **Shawn Walker**
Edited by: **Tumika Cain**

Stay Connected with Us!

Text **LOCKDOWN** to 22828 to stay up-to-date with new releases, sneak peaks, contests and more…
Or CLICK HERE to sign up.

Thank you!

Like our page on Facebook:

Lock Down Publications: Facebook

Join Lock Down Publications/The New Era Reading Group

Follow us on Instagram:

Lock Down Publications: Instagram

Email Us: We want to hear from you!

Submission Guideline.

Submit the first three chapters of your completed manuscript to ldpsubmissions@gmail.com, subject line: Your book's title. The manuscript must be in a .doc file and sent as an attachment. Document should be in Times New Roman, double spaced and in size 12 font. Also, provide your synopsis and full contact information. If sending multiple submissions, they must each be in a separate email.

Have a story but no way to send it electronically? You can still submit to LDP/Ca$h Presents. Send in the first three chapters, written or typed, of your completed manuscript to:

LDP: Submissions Dept
Po Box 1482
Pine Lake, Ga 30072

DO NOT send original manuscript. Must be a duplicate.

Provide your synopsis and a cover letter containing your full contact information.

Thanks for considering LDP and Ca$h Presents.

DEDICATION

This book is dedicated to my precious, beautiful baby girl, the
love of my life, 3/10.

This shit is as real as it gets. Based on a true story.

ACKNOWLEDGEMENTS

I would like to thank the Boss Man and C.E.O of LDP, Cash.
Thank you for this opportunity. Your wisdom, motivation and
encouragement are appreciated. Thanks, bruh.

To the Queen and C.O.O of LDP, thank you for all that you do,
sis. Your hard work, dedication and loyalty to this company
never goes unnoticed.

The grind is real. The loyalty in this family is real. I'm riding
with LDP 'til the wheels fall off. Go hard or go home!

Ghost

Chapter 1

It was a peaceful Saturday evening in our household, for a change. My father had been M.I.A. for an odd number of days, but it didn't cause us any concern. For once, we could relax and breathe easy without the feeling of my father's deadly presence lingering about.

Me, my mother, my sister, Mary, and my brothers, Gotto and Juice, were sitting in the family room watching a DVD movie on the television. My eyes and ears were glued to the action on the screen when I heard the unmistakable sound of the front door opening and closing. It slammed with an ominous bang, causing me to immediately go on alert.

Damn, this nigga always on some bullshit, I thought to myself, heart pounding nervously.

Over the years, I had learned to detect the slightest sign of this nigga's anger. A slammed door, prolonged silence, a slight scowl—numerous things hinted at a foul attitude, which had always been followed by violent displays of his torrid temper.

I glanced over at my mother. She sat there, shoulders slumped, dominated by a profound sadness, awaiting the torture that was sure to come. As for Juice, his attention remained on the movie. I shuddered as soon as my father invaded our space with a whole lot of anger coming off of his brow.

"Waddup, Pops," I spoke, hoping to lighten his attitude before it erupted into a full-blown tornado.

I had no idea what his problem was today, but it never took much for him to go on a muthafuckin' rampage. And the half empty bottle of Jack Daniels in his hand, was another reason I feared what was to come. He ignored my greeting and glazed at Momma.

"Bitch, come here!" He took a long swig from the bottle before twisting the cap back on it. I looked from him to Momma and saw the terror in her eyes. She seemed to be stuck between obeying him and balling up into herself. She must've chosen the latter because, like a child, she wrapped her arms around her shoulders and bit down on her bottom lip.

"Bitch, I said bring yo muthafuckin' ass here! Now!" My father slung the whiskey bottle at the television with all of his might. *Wham!* The flat screen exploded and it fell off of the wall and crashed to the floor. Juice jumped. Momma screeched. My lips curled up. We all knew he was just getting started

He walked up to my mother, snatched her by the throat, lifting her off the couch and into the air with one swift motion.

"Bitch, whenever I tell you to come to me, you bring yo monkey ass here!" he threw her to the floor, straddled her and smacked her across the face so hard.

Whap! Whap!

What did I do?" she screamed. "K.O.! K.O.! Please, baby, don't do me like this! Please don't beat me in front of our kids! I ain't do nothing! I promise I didn't!" Cries of anguish and despair escaped the beautiful lips of a woman who rested a terrifying gaze upon the man who stood before her. The same man whose job was not only to provide for their family, but to protect them.

"Please, Daddy. Nooo." Mary cried, her voice, barely above a whisper. She knew, like I did, that interfering could cost us our life.

He raised his hand with lightning speed. *Smack!* His hand thunder clapped across her face, causing her to slightly lose consciousness. "Bitch, you belong to me! If I wanna whoop yo monkey ass every single day for the rest of your life, I will. You *my* bitch, and I do whatever the fuck I wanna do to *my* bitch. I don't give a fuck who's watchin'!" He stood up, reached down and drug her across the floor by her hair, all the way from the living room, past the dining room and into the kitchen. "Wake up, bitch!" With that, I heard him strike her once again, as her cries and pleas fell upon deaf ears.

A solemn tear rolled down my cheek; my body looked calm compared to how tangled my mind was, though. I hated when my old man beat on my mother. It was something that I could never get used to even though it happened almost every single day.

My father was a brutal man with a quick temper and a short man complex standing 5 feet 7 inches tall, and built like a bull. It seemed like he took pride in beating my mother, often times for reasons that he created in his own head.

I could not wrap my head around this shit. What man, in his right mind, could put his hands on a woman? The same, delicate woman who carried yo seed for 9 months, nurtured them to the best of her ability and did the best she could by yo ignorant, lying, cheating ass. That was some straight bullshit and I was tired of it.

Damn, Momma. If only I could help you some way, somehow, I thought to myself feeling defeated.

My older brother, Juice, stood on the side of me looking toward the kitchen where he could see my father on top of our mother. "Fuck! I don't feel like hearin' her do all that mutha-fuckin' screamin' today. That shit gets irritatin' after a while. Pops need to start whoopin' her ass in they room." He waved them off and started to pick up the fallen TV.

I gave him a menacing look. I just knew this fuck boy would grow to be like the coward ass of a man we shared our DNA with.

Our mother was in the kitchen getting the shit beat out of her, and this nigga dismissed it, yet at the same time, condoning it. I walked over toward the kitchen to get a better view, but ensured I stayed a great distance away, as to not draw attention my way.

"Bitch, why you come home 20 minutes late, huh? You cheatin' on me? You fuckin' some other nigga, huh? Don't you know I own yo ass?" He wrapped his hands around her neck, cutting off her only source of oxygen.

I watched her struggle to release the strong grip he had around her neck, as she continued flailing her legs.

Damn, Momma, I want to help you so bad, but who would comfort you in his absence, if something happened to me?

Tears welled up in my eyes, threatening to escape, as I watched the horrific scene play before me.

"If I gotta kill you to get you to understand, then so be it." She tried her best to get him up off of her, but to no avail. He cocked his head back, laughing derisively enjoying the sight of my mother squirming beneath him.

My baby sister, Mary, scurried into my arms, her body trembling with fear. I held her like I did every time we had to endure our father beating our mother.

With my arms around her tightly, I felt her body mold into mine. Her heart beating like a drum into my chest, her innocent brown eyes filled with apprehension. She held onto me for dear life, being that out of my other brothers and I, it was me who provided her with a safe haven. I was her security blanket. As long as I was around, she had someone to comfort and protect her.

"Taurus, he gon' kill momma this time. There is blood everywhere, and she can't breathe. What are we gonna do?" she whimpered, laying her little head onto my stomach, shaking uncontrollably.

I was 14 years old, trying to figure shit out and protect my 9-year-old sister from the cards life had dealt us, but always coming up empty handed. My father was a cold man, so we never were naïve enough to think, for one second, that he wouldn't do us the same way he did Momma, although he never attempted to. How in the hell was I going to protect Mary and help our mom without putting myself on the receiving end of our father's wrath?

"We ain't gon' do shit. That ain't our problem." Juice said, assessing the damage of the television. He looked it over and then shook his head. "Fuck! Where we gon' get another TV? This house lame as fuck anyway."

Juice never concerned himself with our parent's affairs. Hell, he approved of what our father did to our mother on a daily basis. Put simply, Juice didn't give a fuck about no one, but Juice. If it wasn't about getting money or getting pussy, then it didn't concern him.

"A *fuckin'* TV?" I moved my sister out of the way and walked toward my 17-year-old brother. He stood in his boxers with no shirt, his long dreadlocks flowing down his back. "Nigga, you worried about a TV when our mother in there getting her ass killed?" I was getting heated, and a little disgusted by him.

He shrugged his shoulders. "I don't give a fuck! Long as he ain't whoppin' my ass then I couldn't care less. She shouldn't have come home late. That ain't got nothin' to do with neither one of us. A woman supposed to get her ass whopped if she ain't honoring her man. That's how Pops raised us, and that's how shit gotta go. Otherwise, the house be fucked up, and we can't have that." He looked me up and down. "Nigga, what you huffin' and puffin' fo? You betta get yo extra swoll ass up outta my face before I whoop yo ass like he whoopin' hers."

Before I could even think to stop myself, I swung and punched Juice right in his jaw. *Bam*! I got tired of him that nigga speaking ill about our momma, disregarding her essence of a woman, acting as if she was pure trash. That shit grinded my gears. He fell backwards right onto the glass table, spewing shards of glass everywhere. "Punk ass nigga, that's my momma in there you talkin' about!" *Bam*! My fist collided with his cheek, as he stumbled to stand to his feet; knocking him back down.

My sister screamed. "*Ahhhhhh*, y'all stop fightin'! Please stop fightin'!" She tried to pull me backward, but my little brother, Gotto, grabbed her, lifting her up into the air.

"Fuck that! Let them niggas fight. That's how we get down in this family." Gotto said, as he slung her onto the couch. "Fuck that nigga up, Juice! You supposed to be the oldest. Right now, you lookin' like a pure bitch!"

My sister, Mary tried to run back over to us to break up what was about to transpire. "No, y'all don't need to be fightin'. Y'all supposed to be…"

Smack! Gotto open-handed her with his right, causing her to lose balance and tumble backwards onto the couch, before sliding to the floor. He reached down, grabbing a handful of her hair, "Shut the fuck up! You are a girl! Speak when spoken to." He raised his hand in an attempt to strike her again, when I intercepted, jabbing him right in his left eye, tackling him into the wall with a loud *Doom*!

Being that the wall was so thin, we managed to fall through, ending up in the closet of the adjacent room, covered in drywall. I straddled him and smacked him across the face like a bitch. "Fuck nigga, you think you finna be putting yo hands on my sister, you got anotha thing comin!" I slapped him again and he spit blood into my face.

"Fuck you, Taurus! Fuck you and that bi-!"

Bam! Before he could finish, I kneed him in the nuts, connecting my right fist to his jaw. *Crack*! "Nigga, I swear to God, if you ever put yo hands on my sister again, Imma-"

I was in such a rage, I didn't even hear him come up behind me. Juice punched me in the back of the head so hard that I bit my tongue. Blood filled my mouth, the pain blinding. He grabbed me around the neck, pulling me back into the living room. Picking up the flat screen TV, he brought it down over my head dropping me to the floor.

I struggled to get up. Mary jump onto his back, punching him on the side of the face. "Leave my brother alone, Juice! You always picking on somebody!" She yelled out, before biting into his cheek.

"Aaarrrggghh, you bitch!" he flipped her over his head and onto me, knocking the wind out of my body for a few seconds. "Imma kill you and that bitch ass nigga!" he picked up a shard of glass from the floor and yanked the curtains from the window, wrapping it around the glass with his back toward us.

Struggling to get to my feet, I darted towards his back at full speed and kicked him right in the nuts. He dropped the glass immediately and I got to punching him repeatedly in the back of his head until he curled up into a ball.

Gotto jumped on my back, causing my knees to buckle, sending me down to the floor. Though he was 5 inches shorter than me he was 50 pounds heavier. He punched me all over my head and neck, repeatedly. "Hoe ass nigga, get off my brother! You don't put hands on him for no bitch!"

His punches were fucking me up. I mean, them muthafuckas hurt. All I could do was cover my head like Juice did because his fat ass was sitting on my back. From the corner of my eye, I saw Mary unplug the lamp that sat on the table right next to the couch.

As soon as she got it, she ran over and smashed it against my brother's head. Even though I didn't like for her to get involved with anything, I knew that someone hurting me always brought out her protective side. I was all she had, and we both knew it. Neither of us knew what would happen to her if danger came to me. Inside I shuttered to even think about it.

"Get off him you bully!" she said, before climbing onto the couch and jumping down on him with both feet. He hollered out in pain. Climbing onto the arm of the couch, she jumped off it again, this time leading with her elbow.

I crawled over to Juice, aiming my punches at his dome. That nigga rolled over unto his back and grabbed my hands as we continued to exchange blows. All the while, hearing my father in the kitchen still tormenting our mother. Gut-wrenching sobs escaped our mother's lips.

Fuck! He had that extension cord!

Even though we weren't in the same room, the swoosh of the cord slicing through the air could be heard over our ruckus. We'd heard it enough in the past to recognize the sound.

"Please K.O! Stop, baby! I'm begging you! Please! Please!" The sounds of wailing and suffering echoed throughout the house.

The cord whipped through the air in loud zips before connecting with her flesh. "Bitch, you belong to me! If I gotta kill you to get you to understand that then so be it!" He yelled.

I knew that this was all I'd ever been exposed to, but inside I longed for something more. Just a little peace. Truthfully, I didn't even know if what I longed for even existed, because I had certainly never seen it with my own eyes.

Mary started punching Juice in the back when our front door flew open and my uncle, Li'l James, came into the house and dropped his 40-ounce can of beer.

Chapter 2

My uncle, Li'l James, had moved down from Chicago to stay with us after getting himself nearly killed twice the summer before trying to run into two different dope spots. The first one left him shot in the shoulder and his homies had to drag him to the car after they killed the three people inside; and the second botched robbery got him shot twice in the back. Trying to change his life, he decided to follow my father to Memphis where he could go to school, and pursue his dream of becoming a Chef. But, after residing in Memphis for about three months, he started working under my father, selling huge quantities of heroine. I'm not entirely sure what ever happened to his motivation to become something other than the hood norm. He was a light skinned, slim man, standing 6 feet even. He and my father had the same mother, but different fathers.

Running into the living room, he pulled Mary off of Juice, then leaned down and tried to pry us apart. "Aye, you l'il niggas stop alla this muthafuckin' fightin'. Y'all supposed to be brothers. This fuck nigga shit right here."

As soon as he did, Juice got up and kicked me in the stomach, making me throw up a little bit. "Fag, get yo bitch ass offa me." He turned to our uncle. "And you don't tell me what to do because you ain't my father! If you put yo hands on me Imma fuck you up, too."

"Oh yea?" my uncle said as he shoved me to the side, stepping toe to toe with Juice. "What you say you gon' do, l'il nigga?"

Squaring up, Juice got into a boxing stance with a busted lip and his nose bleeding profusely. "You heard me, nigga. Imma…"

Awk! Li'l James yanked him up by the throat, raising him to the air.

"I don't know who the fuck you think you talkin' to, but you betta come correct when you talkin' to me. I ain't nan one of them fuck niggas in the streets."

Desperation to breathe overtook him, and Juice tried to peel Li'l James' fingers from around him. Quickly jumping to my feet, I ran to the closet to retrieve my father's baseball bat, a wooden Louisville Slugger.

When I got back into the living room, Mary was on her knees, with pleading eyes, crying hysterically. "Please let him go, L'il James!"

Planting my feet firmly, I swung the bat with all my might, slamming it into my uncle's back. *Wham!* I reloaded, bringing it down on him a second time. *Wham!* "Pussy, let my brother go!" I cocked back to strike again, but he dropped Juice and fell unto his knees.

I respected my uncle to a fault, but I wasn't with that shit. I didn't give a fuck how much my siblings and I fought each other, wasn't nobody else finna come and put they hands on neither one of us. That shit wasn't happening. I loved my siblings and would bury a muthfucka six feet deep when it came to them.

L'il James crawled across the floor and as I was about to whack his ass again, when I heard my father holler out. "This bitch dead! I'm killing this bitch! Imma find a new woman."

Instantly dropping the bat, I darted to the kitchen just in time to see my father hovering over my mother with his foot to her neck, looking down on her with hatred in his eyes. The feeling of nauseousness consumed my body, as tears blurred my vision, and the realization of the dilemma I was faced with clouded my mind. Helping my mother could cost me my life, but I was paralyzed with fear. One wrong move, could end me, her, us all.

Truthfully, I was fucking terrified! I knew, but then again, I didn't know what my father was capable of. That thought alone had me shook, so all I could do was wrap my little sister into my arms tightly, as we cried together.

"Taurus, you gotta save her. You can't let him kill our mother. Please." Mary whimpered.

Nodding my head, I took a deep breath, preparing myself to go at him full speed, when my uncle pushed me out of the way, bolting toward my father, tackling him into the stove, catching him off guard. My father went on a rampage and started punching my uncle all in his head. *Bam! Bam! Bop! Bop!* One fast blow after the next, my father hit him. Falling off of him, Li'l James picked him up and slammed him onto the kitchen floor, directly on his back. He crashed into the floor with a loud thud!

"Nigga, you got to be out yo rabbit ass mind comin' between me and mine!" My father hollered into his face before kicking him so hard in the chest that he flew backward against the refrigerator. He knelt down and punched him directly in the mouth, grabbed a plate from the cabinet and broke it over his head.

Meanwhile, my mother laid on the floor, unmoving. I started to panic. I wanted to check on her to see if she was still breathing. The tears cascaded down my cheeks. I tried my best to see if her chest had risen and fallen, but to no avail. She laid on her back in the middle of the kitchen with her eyes closed.

Please, Momma. Please. Don't leave us. We need you. My mind was racing.

Mary dropped down to her knees, and pushed my mother's hair out of her face. "Mom, are you okay? Please say something to me. I'm worried about you." She cried with tears dripping off her chin. I could see her trembling in fear as she checked on our mom. No kid should ever have to endure the things my siblings and I had.

My father broke another plate over L'il James' head. "Bitch nigga!" Lookin down on Mary, he said, "Get that bitch up and the both of y'all go in that bathroom and wash y'all selves. When

I get back, I want the both of y'all clean, and in bed." Mary too afraid of my father to do anything else, nodded. "Juice, you and Taurus come with me. I'm gon' show y'all what it means to fuck in my bidness. Gotto, when they get out of the bathroom, you go in there and get yo'self together then I want you in the bed. You too soft to come with us." He pushed my sister out the way. "Bitch, get yo ass up, now!" He slapped my mother across the face. "Bitch, get yo ass up and get in that bathroom, now!"

She couldn't move, no matter how hard she struggled to do so. Seeing her have such a hard time breathing, solidified the hatred that had developed in my heart over the years for this man.

As much as I wanted to kill the nigga for constantly putting his hands on my mother, I was thankful that she was still alive.

Her face was barely recognizable, looking as if she'd been stung by bees. Even her lips were swollen and disfigured. She struggled to come to a standing position. In a show of defiance to the man who sired me and a simultaneous act of love to the mother who birthed me, I helped my mother stand up. She did on wobbly knees, too wounded and embarrassed to look any of her children in the face. I didn't care what my father would have done to me for helping her. It was the least I could do.

My father smacked L'il James across the face again, causing blood from his mouth to scatter across the wall. "Juice, grab this nigga leg, and Taurus, you grab the other one. We finna take him down to the basement."

"Nall, K.O., come on, big bro. Don't do me like this. Please, man."

Juice smacked him with a skillet, knocking him out cold. *Clung!*

"Bitch nigga, shut up and take what you got coming to you like a man. You should have kept your nose out of family biz." My father opened the door and we literally drug him down the stairs to the basement.

I watched his head bounce off every step. When we finally got to the bottom landing, we drug him across the floor, and then my father picked him up, and Juice and I held him against the wall while my father hit him repeatedly with a hay maker. Watching my father treat his *own* brother like scum, confirmed my thoughts. This man was a savage and he wasn't gonna take shit from *nobody*!

Whoom! "Bitch nigga, I told you to never get in my business." *Whoom!* "That's my bitch up there, and if I wanna whoop her ass every single day for the rest of my life, Imma do it." *Whoom! Whoom! Pit! Pat! Whoom!* He started punching and slapping him so fast, my eyes could barely keep up.

Before I knew it, my uncle was hunched over with thick globs of blood pooling from his mouth, looking like red slime. His teeth were all around his feet, and his jaw was twisted weirdly. He tried to speak, but his words were not legible.

My father grabbed a long screwdriver out of his toolbox. "You see this bitch nigga right here put a black eye in the game by trying to stand in between me and the discipline of my woman. For that, the penalty can only be death, and its gon' be the bloodiest death y'all gon' see for the rest of your lives. If either one of you ever cross me, this is going to be your fate. I won't hesitate to take you out the game. You niggas belong to me. You came out of my dick. I brought you into this world and I'll torture you all the way out. You niggas understand?"

We both nodded. I had never been more afraid of anybody in my entire life. I felt trapped, alone, and vulnerable. And on top of that I was worried about my mother upstairs.

"If I'll kick the shit out of the woman that I love, what the fuck you think I'm finna do to him?" he said, with a crazy look in his eyes.

Juice and I knew better than to give him a response. Our job was to do exactly what we were told. My father answered himself when he leaned back and came forward with the screwdriver fast, jamming it right into my uncle's face. I could feel the vibration of it breaking through his skin. All Juice could do was look on it amazement, as if he'd been put into a trance.

This nigga is a fuckin' psychotic maniac, I thought to myself. *Karma always come back ten-fold.*

"Arrggh! Shit! Arrggh! Shiiittt! Heelllppp meee!"

His blood splattered across my face, feeling hot to the touch. He tried to struggle against the binds, so I held him more firmly.

My father slammed it into his face repeatedly, until his head hung over his chest. I had so much blood on my face that it felt like somebody had poured hot spaghetti sauce over the top of my head.

"Drop that bitch nigga! Juice, go get that axe, and hurry up."

My brother damn near broke his neck grabbing the weapon and coming back. After putting it into my father's hands, we were instructed to lay Li'l James out on the concrete, and one by one, we watched the horror of his limbs being severed.

The whole time, I stood there perplexed. Confusingly enough, I was sick to my stomach and yet fascinated at the same time. The craziness of it all excited me, and I started to watch all giddy like.

After my father cut off his arms and legs, he placed them in a plastic bag that was triple layered. Then we took him outside and dumped him in the big metal garbage can where my father had Juice and I douse him with a whole gallon of gasoline before lighting him on fire. "Burn muthafucka, burn! You niggas ever cross me this gon' be your fate!"

I had no doubt in my mind that the nigga was as heartless as they came. It was his way or no way, either way, he wasn't taking no L's.

After we set him ablaze, my father let him burn for four hours straight. The first murder, happened right before my eyes, and I felt helpless. I had to get from under him.

We poured his ashes into another big black bag where we took sludge hammers, crushing the rest of the bones that didn't disintegrate to ashes. We loaded into my father's truck and drove to the creek where we dumped his remains into the water.

As we watched the creek swallow what was left of my uncle, Li'l James, I couldn't help, but feel slightly frightened of my old man. He was a force to be reckoned with.

"I'm gon' build a dynasty out of one of you l'il niggas, but y'all gotta be killas. You can't let nothing stop you from getting ahead, not even your own blood." He spit to the side of him, then turned to me and Juice. "Now, one of you is going to kill the other 'cause there can be only one after me. Deep in my heart, I know which one." He shook his head. "In order for us to get to where we need to be, one of you l'il niggas to be fearless. I want y'all to hate each other, and to hate anybody outside of you. Fuck being weak! I'll kill both of you l'il niggas if I ever detect any pussy in you. You got that?"

I heard every word loud and clear, but I couldn't get my mother of my mind.

Ghost

Chapter 3

I really couldn't grasp what he was talking about at that age, but something in me told me that I had to be ready for a lot. I didn't know what I was mentally preparing for, but I just felt in my heart of hearts that it was going to be something life altering.

Releasing our necks, and frowning up his face, my father pushed on me, then Juice. "Juice, I want you to whoop your brother ass. I mean fuck him up, right now!" he demanded, pushing Juice in my direction.

I swallowed hard, feeling like I had to shit. I got the bubble guts, and started farting like a muthafucka. The last thing I wanted to do was fight my brother. Juice had hands, and what I mean by that is that he was a beast when it came to fighting. I was just learning how to get down.

I didn't want to fight my big brother out of love for him, but out of fear as well. The situation with our mother, took me to a different place in my mind, and when he showed absolutely no respect for her, I lost it. I didn't play when it came down to her and Mary. That fear shit went right out the window.

Juice paused looking at me. He took a deep breath and looked over at my father before putting his guards up. "Put up your dukes, Taurus, let's just get this over with."

My Father snapped, "What the fuck you giving him a chance to do that for? Get yo ass over there and fuck him up, or Imma fuck you up, royally!" He threatened, with his chest heaving up and down.

I swallowed again, in that moment hating my father for making us do this. Before I had the chance to put my guards up and throw my first punch, Juice rushed into me, whacking me three times, aiming at my chest and stomach.

It knocked the wind out of me, sending me down to my knees,

struggling to breathe.

"Juice, go in there and fuck him up, now!"

I tried to get up off of that knee, but there my brother was again. He picked me up and slammed me on my back onto the unyielding concrete. I blacked out. When I awoke, he was standing over me in our bedroom with tears in his eyes. I wanted to know how I made it back into the house because I didn't remember anything after getting slammed.

"Yo, I ain't mean to whoop yo ass like that, l'il brother, but you know how Pops get when he mixes that crack with his weed. Them primos be having him all fucked up. He would have probably beat me into a bloody pulp had I not did what I did to you."

I immediately grew lightheaded when I attempted to sit upright in the bed.

Juice and I shared a room, and Mary and Gotto shared one, being that my father felt like Gotto was his second daughter simply because of how *soft* he was. Gotto cried about everything, and due to that, he received shitty treatment from our father.

I never could understand why my father was extremely hard on us, to the point where we never knew whether he genuinely loved us, or if he felt trapped by our mother, so he dealt with us.

I felt bad for us all. Juice living in our father's shadow to please him, Gotto being overly sensitive because that was his nature, Mary not knowing what a male role model truly was, me for having to take on adult responsibilities, and my mother for be trapped in this loveless, controlling, abuse ass relationship, where her next breath of air wasn't guaranteed.

I told Juice that I was thankful he didn't fuck me up the way he could have. I had seen him screw some cats over in the streets, and the fact that my middle only hurt a little bit and there was no damage to my face, was a blessing.

My mother was a real quiet, beautiful woman that liked to stay to herself. She didn't have many friends, and the few that she did have, my father always found a way to piss them off because he scrutinized them so closely, killing their desire to want to come around. In truth, I think he ran them off because he couldn't handle her having anyone outside of him.

Deep down, I think he knew he treated her like shit and was afraid she'd come to her senses and leave him. Her Creole and black heritage attracted him to her with her fair skin, silky hair, and curvy body, but he'd get jealous with all the attention she drew. I can't count the times he'd come home and beat her ass because his ego got bruised. I never understood that shit. Why get with a pretty woman if you couldn't handle others admiring her looks? Instead, it was like he tried to beat the beauty out of her. When I'm real honest with myself I'd admit that our father wasn't shit and he definitely didn't deserve our mother.

She had one best friend, by the name of Shaneeta, that came around nearly every day regardless of what my father said to her. She had moved from Chicago a year after we did. Back in Chicago, her and my mother had been best friends all throughout high school. She was caramel skinned, about 5 feet 3 inches tall, and thick as a peanut butter sandwich. Her tongue was sharp. Her personality was jazzy, and uncut. She let you know exactly what was on her mind at all times, and she didn't care how you felt about it. We enjoyed having her around because was the only one that refused to take any bullshit from my father.

One day, my old man decided to take Juice and Mary to some concert in Orange Mound. He rarely ever did anything nice for us. Juice had begged him for months about the concert. I assumed, he granted Juice his wished, being that he kicked my ass real good not long ago. Gotto had chosen to spend the night at one of his friend's houses, leaving me and my mother alone at home. I always enjoyed alone time with my mother, simply because it was the only times I knew without a shadow of a doubt, that she was safe and sound from harm.

Unbeknownst to me, Shaneeta came by that night to check in on my mother, but she hadn't made it home from work yet. She rang the doorbell and I could see that it was her, because we stayed on the first floor and had a window that overlooked the porch.

I opened the door and she asked me where my mother was. I told her that my mother had not made it back home from work, but that she would be there in less than an hour. Instead of her saying that she would come back later, she stepped pass me into the house. The scent of her perfume went up my nose, enticing me.

"Where yo evil ass father at?" she asked, looking around the house as if she were a fine ass probation officer. She had on a tight summer dress with some flip flops that showcased her perfectly pedicured toes.

Sizing her up, I began to feel somewhat uncomfortable. This visit from her in particular, felt different. I could tell she was up to something. After all, she was a grown woman, and I was just a teenager. She intimidated the hell out of me.

"He took Mary and Juice over to Orange Mound. They having a concert over there or something. I think Ball and MJG performing."

She smiled, nodding her head. "And where is that other boy at, uh, Gotto?" She raised her eyebrows.

I ran my hand down my long, black and gray, beaded French braids, matching my Jordans and Polo fit. Mary always helped me swap the beads out to ensure the style matched with every outfit I wore, being that I was real anal about clothes already, and had to stay fitted at all times.

"He spent a night at his friend house."

She ran her tongue across her juicy lips. "So that means you're the only one here?" She lowered her eyes, and walked up to me.

28

I was still standing by the door, and the closer she got to me the more my eyes bulged out of their sockets, causing me to blink a few times. It felt like it was getting hotter in the crib, and the more I inhaled the intoxicating scent of her perfume, the harder my dick got. Everything in me said run, but the head below my waist kept me frozen. She pushed me against the door, and sucked on my neck.

"I always wanted to fuck one of my best friend's sons. Y'all are some handsome l'il men, and I like you the most because you got those cute ass dimples." She kissed each one of them, and then licked my neck before reaching between us and squeezing my dick. "I wish I had men as fine as y'all walking around my house. I'd be letting y'all fuck me all the time. Look at how hard this young meat is." She moaned in my ear with a death grip on my dick.

I was a little afraid at first, but once I felt my mans down low rise to his full length, all that shy shit went out the window. There was no denying it, Shaneeta was fine as a muthafucka, but I had never looked at her in a sexual light, and wasn't sure whether this feeling was wrong or right. Never had I had sex before, but for some odd reason, I had to have her and was ready to discover what sex was all about. I'd watched Juice take down a few broads, and peeped the happiness he displayed after. Shit, I was ready to be happy, too, and I was glad that she was willing to make me smile.

She dropped down to her knees, pulling the top of her dress down, exposing her B-cup titties that had nipples so big, they looked like they belonged on baby bottles. They were already erect, but she helped them reach their full potential by pulling on them more.

"I'm about to suck yo dick, Taurus, and you bet not tell no-body how I get down. I'm doing this because you my l'il mans, and I wanna teach you about life through this pussy." She explained, reaching under her dress, sticking her hand between her legs, and bringing them up to my full lips. "Taste this salty shit. If you can fall in love with the way a woman taste, then you can master her on every level. The key to most women is through their vagina. You master that, along with their mental, and they will be your slave."

She slowly unzipped my Polo shorts, pulling them all the way down to my ankles. Once there, she pulled my boxers down and my dick sprung up like a flagpole.

"Damn, baby, you're ready for me, huh?" She cooed, looking at my manhood in amazement. I could tell the length and thickness caught her off guard. I was beyond blessed down below.

I was a little worried because I didn't know if my dick was big enough to satisfy a grown woman, but she definitely didn't have any gripes. The next thing I knew I was slidin' into her hot ass mouth while she pumped my dick up and down sucking on the head like it was a chicken bone and she had not eaten in three days. I was all up on my tippy toes with my hands on top of her head.

She tried to talk to me while she was sucking me for dear life, but I couldn't understand nothing she was saying. She had so much spit on my shit that, my piece sounded like wet shoes walking on plastic, as it slid in and out of her mouth. I sped up the pace, and began to feel an unexplainable euphoric feeling. My dick wanted to explode from all of the excitement and attention it was receiving. It was like getting everything you had ever wanted in life, including a million dollars, all on your birthday.

Physically, my entire body started to shake. I hollered out, releasing all of me into her mouth while she pumped my dick back and forth, and licked all over it like she couldn't get enough. Because of its sensitivity, I tried to run away, but she insisted on licking me until she got every drop. She led me to the couch where she sat, and lifted her dress.

"I want you to lick my pussy now, baby. Can you do that for yo aunty?" she asked pulling her panties all the way to the side and showing me her hairy pussy.

She spread her lips, and all I could see was pink. I got down on my knees so fast that I damn near sprained my ankle. She drove her fingers in and out of her box anticipating my tongue, which I gave her right away. I licked up and down her crease like I had seen the men do on the porno movies, beckoning her to open her legs wider.

"Wait, baby, wait, you gotta concentrate on this little piece of meat right here," she said pointing to her clitoris. "Let me pull these lips all the way back for you so you can get what you're supposed to."

And that she did. I saw her clitoris pop out looking like a thick pink nipple. "Now wrap your lips around that, and suck for yo aunty. Please, baby."

As soon as I did that, she screamed so loud that I thought I had broken her pussy, and I didn't even care because that salty taste was so addicting. She wrapped her legs around my head and started humping my mouth, and I kept on going, attacking that clit until she began to shake and cry simultaneously.

Next thing I knew, she was kneeling under me stroking my shit up and down, looking me in eye. "I want you to fuck me now. I'm gon' show you how to really hit this pussy. And I like to be fucked hard. All women do. Don't let hoez fool you. We love our holes to be filled up and beat in, trust me."

After she had me back to full mass, she bent over the couch, smacking her bare ass, before spreading her cheeks. "Come on l'il daddy," she purred, licking her juicy lips. "Make sure you pull on my hair, too, and be sure to rip it out. It's natural so I ain't trippin."

As soon as I went behind her, and started rubbing my dick up and down between her crease, we heard keys jingling in lock. We scrambled to get dressed and escape, but my mother was too fast.

She caught her best friend reaching under the couch to grab her panties, bare ass in the air with both breast exposed, and me hopping on one leg, halfway back into my boxers.

To my surprise she didn't snap out or cause a scene. She stood shocked, but kept her composure. I don't know what she said to Shaneeta about everything that took place that night, but she never confronted me about the situation.

All that night, I waited for my father to come in and whoop my ass, but he never did. I wondered what really went through my mother's mind, but I was too terrified and embarrassed to explain what it was she saw.

Chapter 3

I had a best friend named Tywain, who was four years older than me. We had linked up when I first moved down to Memphis. We attended the same high school, me being a freshman, and bro a senior because he had been held back the last two years. He barely went to school, but the first time I met him, he had saved my ass.

I was glad he had been there. We went to Hamilton High, and all the kids who attended, seemed to be from one slum or another. It was ratchet as hell. The school had plenty bad ass females, whereas the dudes were just haters.

When I spoke, it was like they knew I wasn't from the South and that was their excuse not to fuck with me on any level. I could have sworn my accent pissed them off.

During a usual day in study hall, I was reading over chemistry notes when this fat, black nigga approached me, slamming his hand on my desk.

"Say, mane, what brings yo slick ass down here to the country?"

I paused from what I was doing, to take a look at this fat, black Negro with gold all in his mouth, sweat stains under his arms, and curled my lip.

Quiet as it was kept, I ain't like none of them country niggas neither 'cause they never gave me a chance. They made me out to be some kind of culprit when they didn't know me, but I knew one was gon' try me. But in that moment, I ignored this stud and kept doing me.

I heard him laugh aloud, slamming his hand on table once again. "I said, what brings you down to the country, home boy?"

Now I was irritated, I wasn't gonna let this nigga hang around me like it was sweet. I didn't know if it was 'cause my drawl wasn't as strong as his and it made him assume I was soft, or maybe he thought city niggas in general, were soft. Shit, the nigga probably hated how fresh I dressed, and took note of how them country girls was lovin' a nigga. Either way, I stood up face to face with him.

"Yo, why don't you back up outta my face, bro?" I demanded, daringly.

He looked over his shoulder to see that the class was fully tuned in, instigating with the ohhhs and whuts.

He laughed nonchalantly. "You must not know who the fuck I am, but you gon' find out real quick."

He pushed me with so much force, that I fell over the chair, hitting my head on desk. Crack!

I shot up so fast, the pain never had time to resonate with me, and I stole him in the jaw, then picked up chair, slamming it over his back.

"Ahhhhhhhhhh, fuuckkk!"

The sound was music to my ears. Before I could bring the chair over his back again, somebody tackled me against the desk and I felt a fist to my jaw. I didn't know who it was, but I knew they hit hard as a muthafucka, and I damn sure didn't wanna get hit by them again, in the seconds that thought took, I caught another blow to the side of my head.

Before I could wrap my head around what was taking place, I had four dudes taking turns whooping my ass. All I could do was curl into a ball.

The teacher didn't do shit, and nobody went to principal, whose ass was probably doped up on rock cocaine anyway. I would have laid there if Tywain never came to see what was going on and got right to business.

The attacks on me came to a halt, but I still heard shoes screeching against the floor. Unshielding myself, I look upward to see Tywain fighting all four dudes, fucking them up.

I immediately bounced to my feet and gave him a hand, getting the best of them. They were all screaming for revenge afterwards.

Tywain hadn't known me from Adam, but he held me down like he was my brother, and in less than seven months, that's exactly how I looked at him.

Two days after I got down with Shanetta, Tywain came knocking on my bedroom window. Me and Juice's room faced the back yard, and being that we were on the first floor, that gave Tywain easy access. I was just getting up to take a piss when I heard the knocks.

Pulling back the sheet we used as a curtain, I saw him standing outside looking both ways as if he were paranoid. Opening the window, I asked him what was good.

"Bro, I need to holler at you. Jump out the window and come fuck with me real quick," he said, still looking both ways.

I didn't have the slightest idea what my dude was on, but he looked real paranoid, like he was up to something. Tywain did powder cocaine heavily. He loved tooting that shit. At the same time, he had a habit of fucking with that Lean. Those two drugs didn't mix, because they sent you two different ways. The Lean was a downer, and the coke was an upper. Most times I didn't know what my nigga was on, but I'd always roll with him.

I jumped out the window and we walked to his car that was parked in the alley. As soon as I got in, what he said sent chills down my spine. It caught me completely off guard, and I didn't know how to react.

"Bruh, I just killed that nigga Tim, and his baby momma." He popped open his glove box, and pulled out a .45 automatic. Tim was a nigga that I went to school with, who played on the basketball team. His baby mother was this older chick that stayed out in Black Haven. She sold weed for her brother Blake, who was in the hospital after being shot three times. I personally ain't have no beef with Tim or his broad, but if Tywain bodied them it had to be for a good reason.

"Yo what happened?"

He took the top off of his Sprite and poured the small container of Lean in it. Tywain had only been in Memphis for three years at this time. He was originally from Brooklyn, New York, but had moved out to Memphis with his mother and sister because he was getting into a lot of trouble back in N.Y. He said that he'd caught a reckless endangering to safety case before he left, and had spent from the age of 12 until 15 in juvie.

"Yo, that nigga Tim been owing me $1500 for almost a month now, and Son acted like he wasn't gon' pay me." He took a long swallow from the pop bottle. "About four weeks back, we were over on Crescent, on the side of the row houses shooting dice and that fool stuck up the gamble. Ain't nobody know it was him other than me, because I identified them same ass black joggin' pants that he wore every day. Not only that, but the Jordans he wore had red scuff marks on the back of them. I remember when that shit happened, kid went bananas. He had just bought them joints, and L'il Money was out there ballin' in some red Timbs. Long story short, they almost got to boxing over that, and me and the homies had to break that shit up." He turned up the B.G. and we listened to him spit while Tywain continued.

"Long story short, I was over on Wilson trying to cop some Lean, and I saw that fool coming out of Wilson's Liquor store with his arms wrapped around his baby mother. Now you know me, I don't give a fuck about clapping no nigga, but I try and stay away from hitting up bitches and kids. So, when I went at Son about my chips, it was the nigga's bitch that got to running her mouth. Talking about her nigga ain't gotta pay me shit, and that any money he got goes to her pockets, and that was gon' be that."

He turned the bottle up again, and nodded his head to the music. His eyes got low and he looked as if he were fallin' asleep. After dosing for a full minute, he continued his story.

"I side stepped the bitch and told the nigga to check his broad because this ain't have shit to do wit her. So, imagine my face when the nigga told me that whatever she say goes and that his bitch had already spent my money on a handbag. Yo, word is bond, I don't know what came over me, but before I knew it, I jammed this foe knuckle up to his bitch forehead and splattered her shit all over his white tee. That fuck nigga tried to run, and I hit him three times in the back. It looked like I was shooting a paint gun the way them holes splattered red. Yo, I stood over both of them and emptied my chrome bitch in 'em. Luckily, it wasn't nobody else around or I would've been booked, 'cause a nigga temper got the best of 'em." He lit a cigarette.

I really ain't know what to say. A part of me was fascinated, and wished that I could have seen all of the shit that had taken place. Ever since I witnessed my uncle being killed, I yearned to see it happen again. I wondered if I had enough heart to take a life. I was sure that I did, but then again, I really didn't know. My father said that me or my brother was going to wind up killing each other, and I just wondered that if I didn't have the guts to kill something, it meant my brother would be killing me in the future. That shit terrified me; I wasn't ready to die just yet. Before I could finish my thought process, I felt Tywain pulling the car away.

"What's good, bro? You know I can't go nowhere. If my old man wake up and see I ain't in my room, that fool gon' have a fit."

Tywain looked like he wanted to fall asleep. "Chill, Son, I just wanna show you something." He sped down the alley, after turning the BG CD all the way up. Five minutes later we were pulling up to an abandoned garage.

Tywain waved me over to follow him after he got out of the Mustang. Before I got out I looked up and down the alley. It didn't seem like anyone was around. I saw a stray black cat casually walking down the alley with a big ass rat in his mouth. Its fur was full of patches, as if it had been fighting since birth. I got out of the car, and followed behind Tywain until I was standing beside him in the garage. He knelt down, shining a flashlight, and I damn near jumped out of my skin when I saw the two bodies laid up against one another in the corner of the garage.

I would have never thought he was capable of murder. When he showed up at my crib, his clothes had no signs of any suspicious activity. He never explained to me how he managed to commit this murder alone or if he had any accomplices.

To be honest, either way, I didn't want to know, I didn't care to know. I didn't want to have shit to do with this situation. Hell, me knowing about the shit was bad enough. I had to bounce!

Tywain shined the light on to his face. I could see that he had a real big cheesy smile. "I just wanted to show you what these muhfuckas look like, Son." He flashed the light back on to their bodies. "You see how shorty shit pushed back. Look."

She definitely had what looked like a sewer hole in the center of her forehead. Most of her face had split in half, and there were what I took to be brain fragments, all over her chest, along with blood. It was a crazy sight, but it fascinated me.

Tywain took the female by the arm and pulled her off of Tim. "Now look at this nigga, kid. Yo, I bet Son didn't think he would die tonight, did he?" He started to laugh. "Yo, all it took was fifteen hundred. That nigga had it on him too, because after I bodied they ass, I searched this nigga bitch and came up with seven Gs. Now why the fuck would she be walking around wit all that?" he asked looking me in the eye.

I shrugged my shoulders. "You know shorty move that green, so maybe she was about to re-up." That was the best I could come up with. I was low key ready to get up out of that garage and back to the crib. I wasn't scared or nothing like that. I was more so worried about my old man coming to my room and not finding me in bed. I didn't know what he would do.

Tywain clapped his hands together. "Fuck, you sho right! That bitch did push green for her brother. Yo, we gotta go over to they crib and kick that door in, Boss. They could be holding still, and ain't no sense in them keeping it, I mean with them being dead and all."

I felt like my nigga was tripping and I was trying to find a way to tell him to drop me off at the crib before he did that, without sounding like I was soft or something. I knew he didn't think no shit like that, but still, it was a constant in my mind. I watched him jog back to his car.

"Come on, Taurus, let's go!" As soon as he said that we heard a glass break in the alley, and Tywain upped that .45 lighting quick. Before I could step out of the garage to see what he saw, he pulled the trigger twice, sending off two loud ass booms. Then he took off running.

Walking out of the garage nervously to see where he had gone, I saw he had stopped short in the middle of the alley, hovering over the person he had shot, who was jerking on the pavement. I couldn't see who it was or whether it was a male or a female. All I saw was white shoes, and one of their legs kicking.

I heard two louder ass booms, and saw the fire spit out of the gun. It lit up the entire alley, and left the smell of gunpowder in the air. Tywain jogged back to the car and got behind the driver's seat.

Panicking, I hopped in the car with him and convinced him to drop me off at the crib. Tywain was my boy and all, but I didn't want shit to do with anything he had planned that night. I had my own bullshit to worry about.

That night, Tywain did go to their house, and he found twenty pounds of Dro, an AK47, and two .9 millimeters. He gave me one of the guns the next morning, and promised I'd get five pounds of loud after he showed me how to serve.

Chapter 4

Shaneeta had a daughter that was a year older than me. She was fine as hell and just as thick as her mother. We went to the same school, and she had everybody thinking that we were cousins. Truth be told, I was trying to find a way to hit that pussy. She was a real good girl. Stayed in church, did all of her homework on time, and never was seen in the faces of boys. I dug her style, because on top of all of that she was a dresser and to me there was nothing sexier than a woman that could dress. That shit turned me on like nothing else.

One day as we were coming out of school, one of the older niggas that played football tried to get at her while we were walking together. She shot him down, and he had the nerve to call her a stuck-up bitch. Now even though I wasn't the typical Captain Save-a-Ho, I wasn't feeling this nigga calling her out of her name. That, coupled with the fact that everybody thought we were cousins, made me feel like the stud was calling me a bitch, and I wasn't going for that. As soon as I heard the word come out of his mouth I did a 180 until I was walking in his direction. Shakia tried to grab my arm, but I wasn't trying to hear none of that. I walked straight up to homey and asked him, "What did you just say?"

He must have thought it was a game, because all he did was smirk, and look past my shoulder at her. "Oh, I wasn't talking to you mane. I was addressing that Missy over thur dat act like she too good for ur' boy." He stood about five inches taller than me, and at least 60 pounds heavier.

All of the school buses were in front of the school, and kids were rushing to them. There were a few teachers that came out, I'm guessing to see students off, and I didn't care about none of it.

Pointing to the sky to catch his attention, he stupidly looked up, and took my chance. *Bop!* I punched his obese ass in the neck, catching him off guard. He grabbed his neck and started wheezing for air. I backed handed him with my knuckles, and kicked him in the nuts. As soon as he bent over, I kneed him in the face, causing him to fall on his back holding his broken nose.

"Next time, have some respect for this Queen." Before I could finish the rest of my words I was snatched up by three teachers, and taken to the principal's office. They suspended me for three days, and Pops beat my ass.

I didn't give a fuck though. A part of me was feeling Shakia, and even though I had a l'il thing with her mother, I wanted to make her my girl. I started to look at her different all of the sudden. I couldn't quite explain why. It was just on that day right there, she'd looked so good to me, and I couldn't have no nigga flexing on her in my presence.

Speaking of her mother, two days later while everybody was at school and work, she knocked on the front door, and I let her in. As soon as she walked across the threshold, she pushed me until my back was up against the living room wall. She started sucking all over my lips, and talking to me all dirty like.

"I heard what you did for my daughter, and that shit drove me crazy." She reached and pulled my pajama pants down. I was already free balling with no underwear so my dick sprung out like an elephant's trunk, only browner. She dropped to her knees. "So, tell me, did you do that because you like her? Or did you do it because you like me?"

Before I could answer, she swallowed me whole, gagging a little bit as she pushed me further down her throat. She unbuttoned her blouse and her big titties came bouncing out with the big brown nipples.

I can't remember what my answer was exactly, but what I do recall is me moaning like a bitch when she nipped her teeth over my helmet, sucking me so hard, that I couldn't help coming in rivers. The next thing I knew she was on top of me, guiding me into her hot cave. That shit felt so good, I could have cried. She leaned down and bit my neck, as she bounced up and down on my dick like I was a bouncy house.

"Damn! I knew yo dick would fill me up. Tell Aunty how good her pussy is. Tell me how you like this shit, L'il Daddy!" she hollered, while she rode me like her life depended on it.

I reached around and grabbed her ass, and held on like I was a jockey or something. It was so soft and big. I could feel that muhfucka rippling every time she slammed down on me and took my dick deep into her body.

"Uhh shit! I don't care if you and my daughter fuck around, just keep giving me this young meat. Keep putting that fresh shit in my pussy and we gon' be alright!" She started to shake on top of me, instructing me to pull her nipples, which I did with no hesitation. Every time I pulled on them, I felt her shoot something against my dick that was inside of her. We stayed on that floor for two hours doing everything imaginable.

The sex romp ended with her sucking her juices off of my dick and my thighs. Before we could get up and call it a day, my mother crept into the living room where we were sprawled out, and dropped her work bag on the floor right by our heads. I must have turned bright white from sheer terror. I just knew she was gon' snap the fuck out this time. I struggled to cover myself.

She laughed out loud. "Boy, ain't no sense in you covering yourself up now. I done watched you and her go at it for the last thirty minutes, and I gotta say this damn woman done turned your ass out." She shook her head and walked out of the living room.

I really ain't know what to take from that, but Shaneeta didn't seem like she was bothered at all. She casually rose to her feet, and pulled her dress down. I stood up and she kissed me on the lips. "Taurus, I know you and my daughter about to be fucking around, but she ain't ready for all that I just showed you, so take it easy on her. That girl like you, so I won't stand in the way of that. Just promise me that this dick is partially mine as well. "

I promised her that, and before she left she took my dick out of my pants and kissed it on the head. After the door closed, my mother came into the living room and gave me a hug, before kissing me on the cheek.

"How do you feel, baby?" She rubbed my bare chest, and then laid her head on it.

I didn't know how to feel. I was more or less worried about her telling my father or snapping out, because this was the second time that she'd caught me smashing her best friend in the house. She was rarely so affectionate, so that was throwing me off, too. I knew that my mother was under a lot of stress and that my old man constantly neglected her. He never allowed her to really leave the house unless it was to work, or he was standing right beside her. He was extremely cold to her, and treated her like dirt. I never saw him hug her or show her any kind of natural affection.

I wrapped my arm around her and hugged her tightly, kissing her on the forehead. "I feel okay. I mean I guess." I didn't know how I was supposed to respond to that question. It felt weird even trying to. I mean she had just witnessed me smashing her best friend on her living room floor. How was I supposed to have felt?

She wrapped both of her arms around my waist, and held me tighter. "You smell like her." She exhaled. "I can't believe that bitch got me kinda jealous." She shook her head and then laid it back on to my chest.

I was taken aback by that comment. I didn't know what she meant by it, so I asked, "What are you talking about, momma? Why would you feel jealous of her?"

She shrugged her shoulders after being silent for a brief moment. "You're my baby, she shouldn't be teaching you all of that." She kissed my bare chest, and we heard my father and siblings coming on to the porch. We separated and went into our rooms.

I didn't know what to make of our brief conversation. I did feel some type of way. I felt like I'd hurt my mother. Like I had somehow betrayed her, and led her to think that I cared about her best friend more than I did her when that was not the case. My mother was my heart and soul. I did not love anybody in the world more than I did her. She was my Angel. Out of all of my siblings, I was the one that looked like her the most, all the way to the gap in my upper row of teeth. Me and my mother had a special bond for as far back as I could remember.

That night, my father beat her so bad that he sent her to the hospital. I don't even think there was a reason for it, or if there was I never found out about it. I just remember sitting in my room contemplating killing him in cold blood. I would protect my mother and be everything to her that he was not. I let my mind wonder, until sleep consumed my body.

Juice woke me up in the middle of the night and told me that Tywain had told him about the weed he'd found. He said he wanted in, and he wasn't taking no for an answer. I played the dumb role and acted like I didn't know what he was talking about.

He got out of the bed and closed our door. "Nigga, stop playing wit me before I kick yo ass. I don't know why you think I'm so slow. Yo, I know he bodied Tim and Angie over in the alley on Wilson Street. That nigga get to leaning and tell everything to the niggas he trust. That's gon' be his down fall one day, mark my words."

My mind wasn't on shit he was talking about. I was too busy worried about my mother and wondering if she was okay.

"How can you think about this weed shit when Moms in the hospital all fucked up because of Pops?" I asked, quizzically, getting irritated as hell.

Shit, if it came down to it, I would fight Juice just to prove a point. I felt like he didn't really care about our mother and that was making me feel some type of way.

Juice waived me off. "Bro, she good. Pops said she supposed to get her ass whoop at least once a week. He said that keeps women in check. So, if I was you I wouldn't worry about it."

He sat on the side of bed lookin' down at his feet, putting his foot on the bed, messing with his big toe, looking confused. I hopped out of my bed and stood up looking at him like I wanted to kill him and in that moment, I probably did.

"Whatchu just say, man?" I asked, as my heart pounded through my chest.

Wrinkling his forehead, he looked me over closely, sucked his teeth and he stood up, getting in my face. "Nigga, you heard what the fuck I said! Pops said women are 'spose to get they ass whooped, so he whooped hers. It aint our bizness. When I get my own woman, Imma whoop her ass, too, because that's how its 'spose to be. I wish a nig…"

Whamm! I don't know what came over me, but I swung and busted his lip. With a left and right-hand combo connecting to his chin, I knocked him clean out.

I watched him fall, in what seemed like slow motion. As soon as he did, I stood over him and had visions of blowing his brains out.

Wasn't nobody gon' talk about my mother like that. If he wasn't my brother, he woulda been my first murder. I ain't never been the type to put my hands on a woman.

To me, that's bitch nigga type shit. Only cowards claiming to be men hit women. Muhfuckas that prey on the weak. I could never respect a nigga that bragged about hittin' a female. I never could love my father because he hit my mother so much. No matter how many niggas he killed, and it was a whole lot, I still saw him as soft, and a pure bitch. Men that hurt women and children were lower than scum to me, even back at that age.

That night, my brother and I got into it horribly and he fucked me up. I was gon' pop him with my .9 that I had in my Jordan shoe box, but I let him have that victory for that day.

We wound up plugging in with Tywain, and over the span on 6 months, we served up the Dro game. Weed was the first drug I sold that had me seeing stacks.

Ghost

Chapter 5

As crazy as it sounds, Shakia didn't become my girl until after I turned 17. Around that time, I had been in so much shit, and was going in and out of Juvie. My father acted like he didn't give a fuck. He was too busy focusing all of his attention on Juice, and the heroin empire he was trying to build.

I didn't care. I was doing my own thing. I still went to school as much as possible. I was a thug, but I still wasn't trying to be no dummy. I knew I would need my education down the line, so I wasn't gon' play with that. My only downfall was my short temper. I got mad easily, over the smallest things

I was 17 when I copped my first whip. It was a money green 5.0, and it came equipped with 188 spoke diamond cut bullets, all gold. Tywain had a cousin in Buck Town that was a beast when it came to jacking cars.

It didn't matter what kind of whip you told him you wanted, he'd find a way to get it for you. By this time, I had been hustling good and built myself a strong loyal clientele. I had this plug over in Black Haven that sold me pounds of Loud for two gees, but the catch was, if I wanted to continue to get the same deal from her, I had to keep her competition on their heels. Everyone, including her, who gave me information on a mark, needed me to knock 'em down to size. She ain't want me killing them or nothing like that, she just wanted me to cop all of their product, and cash. The deal was that I could keep the cash, and all the product would go directly to her, and she'd always know just what they were holding because most of the licks were in her inner circle.

Shit sounded crazy, but that's just how shorty got down. I made a mental note to never trust her, and to always keep my ear to the street in regard to her. It would only be so long before kats started to see that she wasn't getting hit, but everybody around her was.

The plug's name was Nell, and I'd met her at a Grizzly's NBA basketball game. Shakia was a basketball fan, and her favorite team was the Chicago Bulls. This night they here in town, and some other nigga was supposed to take her, but an hour before the game he'd stood her up. I had come over to her house in the hopes of creeping with her mother that night, but when I got there and posed that question to her, she told me she couldn't because her daughter was in the house suffering from a broken heart. After saying this last part, she poked her bottom lip out as if she were a little kid. She told me that if I could make her daughter feel better that she would pay it forward to me later on that night, and by this time we were doing some freaky shit. I never even knew how much Shaneeta liked to have that ass fucked until about my 17th birthday, but that was another story.

That evening, I went into their living room and slid onto the couch next to Shakia, and wrapped my arm around her. She lowered her head, and continued crying into the arm of the couch as if she were too shy to let me see her face.

Shaneeta came in and knelt down in front of her. "Baby, why don't you tell Taurus what's the matter?" She coaxed, rubbing her thigh and kissing her knee.

Holding her more firmly, I pulled her toward me so that her head laid on my chest. I could smell her hair products, and a hint of perfume. Her scent got my stamp of approval. I also liked the way she felt laying against me. "Shakia, what happened, ma?"

She lifted her head off of my chest and I wiped away her tears with my thumbs. "Greg stood me up. I was supposed to go to the basketball game with him tonight, but instead he gotta do something for his baby's mother." Her tears began to flow again. "I just wanted to see Derrick lose. I miss Chicago and this is the closest I can get to them," she said, speaking in terms of Derrick Rose playing for the Chicago Bulls.

I ain't know who this Greg nigga was, and I didn't feel like it was my place to ask her that. Lately, I hadn't been peeping her so closely. I had been too consumed by her mother's bedroom antics, and trying to get my weight up in the game.

Not only that, but I had taken a shine to fucking with straight Latino broads, because that's the kick that Juice was on. He was always bringing home a girl so pretty that I could not keep my eyes off of her. So, I started to steal plays from his playbook and dip in that Latin pool. Not saying that I couldn't have crushed him with a black woman because I could have with no problem. In my opinion, sistas were the baddest women on earth, and that would never change. A black woman's beauty was second to none.

I rubbed her chin softly while her mother gave me a look that said she wanted me to heal her daughter. "Look, Shakia, I don't know what you got going on with dude or whatever, but I'm finna take you to that game and we gon' do it big. Where was y'all sitting?" I asked looking for a window to flex on this nigga.

She scooted to the side and grabbed her purse out of the corner of the couch, dug her hand inside, and pulled out the tickets. "We're sitting eighteen rows up from the floor, which isn't bad, and quarter center of half court." She looked at the tickets for a long time, and I could see the sadness enter her face. I hugged her and kissed her forehead.

"Don't even trip I got you."

Three hours later we were sitting on the floor right next to the Bulls bench, and she could not stop thanking me. We were so close to the bench that more than once Derrick Rose brushed across her leg as he was taking his seat, or going back on to the floor. Afterward she got his autograph, and a picture. I enjoyed seeing her smile.

We'd just bought the last tickets before we came in, because it was a sold-out event. As we were leaving from the ticket window, Nell and her five year old brother was coming to the window. Shakia wanted to stop and check her phone messages, and I did as well. I wanted to see what was good with my Facebook because I had a couple l'il Latin stalkers that were on my heels.

As I was scrolling down my messages, I overheard the conversation Nell was having with her little brother.

"I'm sorry, bruh, the people ran out of tickets, but I'll take you to the game on Saturday." The L'il fella was devastated. I mean he broke down crying right there in front of everybody. I damn near wanted to give them our tickets because I hated when kids cried. Luckily, I remembered the other tickets that dude had brought for him and Shakia, so after a little arguing with her, she finally allowed me to give the tickets to Nell. When I handed them to her she looked me up and down like I had lost my mind. I stuck my hands up in the air.

"Damn, shorty, why you looking at me like I just tried to steal your tickets or something?"

She was a heavyset chick with a real pretty face. Caramel skin and red hair. She had to be about 5 feet even. "I'm saying, ain't nobody ever just gave me shit fa free, so what's yo agenda, homeboy?" She had a real southern drawl. She spoke properly, but her accent was heavy with flavor.

I liked her style off the rip. I looked her from head to toe and peeped how she was dressed in an all-black and purple Ferragamo fit, with matching Airmax. She had purple diamonds in her ear lobes, and a purple diamond encrusted female Rolex on her right wrist. I nodded my approval of her swag.

"Yo, me and my lady got floor seats, and we were expecting some more of the homies to show up, but they didn't, long story short, y'all can have these tickets."

She stood looking at me for a long time, and then she nodded as if to say good looking. "Check this out, homeboy, you fuck wit that Loud bag?" She pulled out her phone and started doing something on it. What, I couldn't tell. Shakia came over and I wrapped my arm around her shoulder.

I could tell that she was ready to go into the Arena. She wrapped her arm around my waist, and dug her freshly manicured nails into my side. I kissed her forehead. "Hold on, ma." Turning back to Nell. "Yeah, that's my cue shorty."

"Take this number down and since you did me a favor, I'm about to do you a one."

That was how it all began with her. Two weeks later, I was seeing crazy numbers, and her plug was even more looney. My mother always said that when you did a good deed, that the good would eventually come back to you in threes.

That night, after the game, me and Shakia rolled out to the lakefront. Some of the hoods were getting together, and everybody was meeting up there after midnight. We stopped for a bit to eat at Monster Burger, and I noted that she had been quiet for most of the night. She barely touched her food, and she just wasn't herself. I asked her what the problem was.

It took her a while to respond. She shifted in her seat uncomfortably. "I saw Greg at the game." She exhaled, and grabbed her drink from the table, sucking the juice up through a straw.

I didn't know how to react to that because a part of me wanted to go in for the kill. I wanted to flex on that nigga and steal his slot, but I figured that it would have been ill advised, and it would have made me look thirsty, so I decided to take a bit of a more cerebral approach. "Are you okay? Is there anything that I can do for you to make you feel better?"

She shrugged her shoulders. "I don't know, It's not really your problem. I mean the fact that you took me out is more than anything I could have asked for. You've always been so nice to me, and I don't know why." She placed her juice back on the table and lowered her head.

The burger joint was filling up. There were all kinds of teen-agers coming in, peppered with older folks. Most people were paired up with their significant others. I looked around for any familiar faces or enemies, and spotted none. I did see a few flings though, all hugged up with their men as if I wasn't just tapping that ass that week. I couldn't do nothing but shake my head to that.

We were seated in a booth toward the back of the place. I always tried to sit in the back so I could see all who came in. The restaurant had mood lighting, so it was mostly dim throughout.

I reached across the table and took a hold of her small hand. "Shakia, you know you're my peoples. It's my job to protect you, and to shield you from these trifling ass niggas. I mean I know how it is to be a dude, and I gotta be honest wit you, sometimes we ain't right."

She gave me a look that said she understood. "Especially when I ain't giving the pussy up, huh?"

Now I didn't know how to respond to that because first of all I didn't know that she wasn't fucking. As immature as it sounded, she was so strapped that it was hard to imagine her not getting them walls tapped. I would have never bet that she wasn't getting down. "Why you say that?" Was the best I could come up with?

"Because, it seem like every dude wanna fuck me, and when they find out that I ain't giving up the pussy then they slowly back off, until I find out that they screwing somebody else. So I'm guessing that the source of my problems lies in the fact that I am not sexually active the way I should be or the way they want me to be." She blinked and a tear fell out of her eye.

For some reason the emotional side of her made me want to protect her even more. She was doing something to me that other females did not. It was like she was so vulnerable that I didn't want to go in on her in that fashion, because I felt that she should have been protected by me. So I slid around the booth until I was seated on the side of her, and I nested my face into the crux of her neck and kissed it softly. "Shakia, you're a diamond, and most of these dudes aren't familiar with anything other than Cubic Zirconia, fake jewels. It takes a man above standard to see the treasure that lies within you, because you are special. I don't want you thinking that you can keep a man just because you fucking him, that ain't real, because after the pussy is hit, then what do you have? "

"I don't know. What do you have with my mother, because I know you're fucking her?" She pushed me away from her, and gave me a look that said she was hip to my game and that she wasn't falling for it.

That comment threw me for a loop, because I wasn't expecting her to know all of that. I was sure that me and her mom was careful as hell, and as far as I can remember I don't recall us ever being detected by her. She never acted any different toward me at school, or when we had little family functions together, so her comment blindsided me. "Yo moms taught me a lot about the game. That's a good woman right there and I respect her to the fullest. What her and I have done ain't got nothing to do with how I feel about you. "

She smirked her lips. "Oh yeah, and how is that? It's hard to tell that you feel anything about me being that every time I see you, you're with a female that don't look nothing like me, and barely speak the same language t I do." Her gaze met mine. I could tell her heart was heavy. I gave her a look that told her she had my undivided attention. "Do you have any idea how that makes us black females feel to see our men running around with these Spanish girls, or if they aren't Spanish then they're white. Then y'all be jocking them like they're just God's gift to men, and I personally don't think it's cool because where are we supposed to get our self-esteem and self-worth from? So, when you tell me that you feel something for me it's hard for me to believe that."

She went so deep that I felt like I was drowning. I ain't know how to bounce back from that one. All I could do was keep shit real, and let her know what was on my mind. "I been feeling you for a long time, but I ain't had the time to focus in on those feelings because I been out here in these streets, where I don't want you to be. I been ripping and running and living the fast life trying to get my bands up. Them broads don't mean nothing to me, they just pretty, and when it comes to a man, he gone always wanna smash what's pretty. You ain't never seen me trying to wife none of 'em have you?"

She shrugged her shoulders. "And?"

"And what I'm saying is that it's just me playing in the streets, that shit don't mean nothing. Ain't no race of women on this earth finer than the black woman and you are the perfect representation of that. As far as your mother goes, that sista done taught me a lot, and I ain't iust talking about on the sex level, I mean all around the board. Yeah, we get down from time to time, but neither of us are attaching any strings to it. She was the first female I ever got down with, and I don't regret none of what we've done thus far."

She flipped her curly hair over her shoulders. That day she had her hair hanging down in all silky curls. She looked real good to me. Her outfit was a Givenchy designer dress that hugged her tightly in all the right places. Her cleavage was on display, and her mother had not forgot to pass that gene over to her, because those titties were fat and the prettiest shade of caramel. I just loved our women.

"So, what are you saying, Taurus, that you wanna be with me or something? Are you saying you want me to be your girlfriend? Your chick on the side? Your buddy? I mean what? What is going through that big head of yours?" She scratched her arm and looked at it closely. "Damn I just got bit by a Mosquito."

I reached over, rubbing her bite. "I'm saying that I don't know what we should be, but I'm definitely feeling you, and I have been for a long time. I want you to be more than just my friend, but I don't know what that entails."

She sucked her teeth. "Yeah, because you know I ain't finna go for you playing me off for one of those Spanish broads. If we ever decide to become an item I ain't about to allow you to mess with nobody but me. You saying that I'm a Diamond, then I should expect to be treated as such by a man that I know don't mess with fake jewelry. Am I right?"

You know it's crazy when a female can pick up on your game and throw it back at you before you even have the time to see how it sunk in. Shakia was cold at that. She had a habit of taking my words, sucking out the definitions or meaning of where I was going with them, and throwing them back at me to make me practice what I preached. That characteristic alone, blew my mind about her. Shorty was definitely on her shit when it came to us men.

She bucked her eyes and popped her head forward. That made her curls pop, and I couldn't help but smile. "Well?"

"Ain't nothing I can say, ma, because you are exactly right. Which is why I don't want to say I'm mature enough to take that leap, because I'm still out here in these streets, and I will be for a minute."

She lowered her head as if the fight was taken out of her. "Yeah, I figured that. Then, there is still this thing with my mother that would be hard for me to get past. I'd always wonder if you guys were sleeping around behind my back. That would never sit well with me, because I can't compete with her. I don't know the first thing about sex. I would literally be a bore in that department. On top of that, I'm so freaking emotional, and knowing me, I'd fall crazy in love with you and become psychotic. I'd want you all to myself at all times." She shook her head, as if having accepted her fate of being single indefinitely. With saddened, eyes she said, "I don't think anybody will ever love me. Dudes are so hard to be with. And they say us women are complicated."

Speechless, I couldn't help but feel slapped in the face by her complete honesty. Killing her with the truth, was better than soothing her with lies. I wasn't that type of dude.

We left the burger joint and wound up at the lakefront. It felt awkward because for most of the ride we rode in silence. I didn't know what to say, and I guess neither did she, so we just laid back and listened to R. Kelly serenade us through my speakers.

The lakefront was packed. I barely found a spot to park, and the only reason I found it is because somebody was pulling out, so I zoomed into that spot, and dropped my top. Shakia hadn't said a word and I felt that something was really bothering her.

"Yo, what's good, ma?" I asked, rolling a blunt. I needed to get that green in my system because my high was wearing off, and when that happened I got severe headaches, which was the last thing I needed.

Before she responded to me, she got out of my car, slamming the door behind her. I watched her walk toward the beach where everybody was hugged up and blowing their green and cigarettes. The parking lot was so loud, because it seemed like everybody there was blasting their music.

I laid back in my seat and watched her for a minute. I felt that maybe she just needed to take a short walk to clear her mind. So, imagine my surprise when I saw her walk up to a couple that was hugged up overlooking the water, and pull the male's arm.

They started to argue. I couldn't really hear what they were saying. She turned to the female who was popping her neck on her shoulders like she was chewing Shakia out. The next thing I knew I saw Shakia smack the shit out of her. That's when I jumped out of my whip and ran over there. People that were there had them in a circle that I had to fight my way inside.

When I say Shakia was whooping that broad's ass, trust me. She had the girl by the hair punching her over and over again.

"Bitch, I told you that the next time you got in my business that I was going to whoop your ass. I'm tired of y'all thinking its sweet just because I'm quiet." She pulled her to the sand and started pummeling her face.

I thought about pulling her off of her, but I decided against it. Whatever old girl had done to her, she probably deserved the ass whoopin'. I hated when people pulled me off of a kat's ass, interfering with my personal affairs. Often, that made me want to tear into their ass. So, I just let her handle business until the girl got up and took off running down the beach.

Shakia walked up to the nigga and pushed him hard as hell, causing him to stumble backwards. He almost fell but caught his balance. He was holding a bottle of Grey Goose in his left hand. "And you think you can keep on playing on my emotions, but it ain't going down like that. I'm tired of you lying to me all the time."

The nigga walked up on her and looked as if he was ready to slap her or something, and that's when I jumped in and separated the two. I wasn't about to let this dude touch her in no way. I don't care how that made me look, that shit wasn't going down. He tried to reach over me and grab her, and that's when I pushed his ass.

"Hold up, nigga, this ain't that type of party. You ain't finna touch her."

Shakia took her earrings out. "Nall, that's okay, Taurus, I ain't afraid of this nigga. If you think you gone just whoop my ass then bring it on, Greg, because I'm not scared of you. My father whooped my ass damn near every day of my life for no reason at all, and I fought him back until he got it, so what you think I'm gone do to you?"

Hearing her reveal this immediately made me think of my

mother. I couldn't understand why so many dudes thought it was okay to physically, mentally, verbally and emotionally abuse women.

Where was her mother during the times she was abused? I felt obligated to protect her after hearing her speak those words.

Greg was a muscular, cocky dude. He had to be about my height, which is 6 feet 2, and every bit of my weight, and that's in the two hundreds. The nigga was built like he worked out every single day. So, when I imagined him hitting her in any way, I got to thinking about all of the times my father had beat my mother and I felt my blood run hot. I was ready to body this nigga. He reached around me again and got his hand on her dress.

"If this nigga move, I'll kick your…"

Boop! I completely blacked out. Eight blows real fast, with four of them landing directly in his mouth, and the last one hitting his chin, knocking him completely out. He fell asleep on his feet, and before he could hit the ground, I scooped him up, dumping him on his head in the sand. That fool didn't move, and I prayed that he did because I wanted to get in his ass.

I got to imagining he was my father and Shakia was my mother. Before I knew it, I had reacted and he wound up on the receiving end. After I knocked his ass out, I threw my arm around Shakia, possessively. "Yo, from now on this me right here. Any muhfucka got something to say about that just know I'm willing to knock a nigga head off over her, that's my word."

I don't know where that fool Tywain came from, but the next thing I knew the homey stepped out of the shadows holding an AK47.

"Everybody heard my nigga, right? Right, matter fact, party over!" He pointed the AK in the sky and let off about twenty shots. Everybody scattered except me and Shakia. That night before she got out of my whip, she leaned over and tongued me down for like three minutes. I'm talking that loud ass, spitting exchanging kissing that leaves a man with a hard dick, and a woman with a wet pussy.

"You better had meant every word that you said, because I'm not gon' play about you. "

I didn't know if I did or not, but I knew that I wanted her to be my woman. There was definitely a bond there and I wasn't about to let nobody hurt her if I could prevent it.

Ghost

Chapter 6

My father had a long table that he'd brought down to the basement for the purpose of board meetings. Any time there was some official business that we needed to know about, he would call a meeting and let us know what the deal was.

He was still in the beginning stages of building our family's empire. I look back on things now and I can say that I never understood what he was really doing in that moment, but it had to have been deep if he'd got it to where we were all millionaires five years afterward.

My old man was extremely strategic. He never allowed for anybody to know what he was fully on because he didn't trust anybody other than himself. I really wasn't paying close attention to my family, because I was doing my own thing.

My father kept on telling us to be patient, and that when the time was right he'd let us know. He said at that time that we were in the beginning stages of wealth and power, but that we needed to eradicate our foes. I remember that being a line that Tupac used back in the day in one of his songs.

So, this particular day, I came down to the basement and around the table sat twenty people. There was one seat open that I took to be mine. Also, there were about thirty dudes standing around the table in black wife beaters. They looked like they just got out of prison, and took a swim in a pool of baby oil.

I came in and took my seat, noting that my father was clearly irritated. I didn't really care because I had to smoke a blunt before I came down there. I knew it was going to be a long day, and once you got down there he didn't expect you to leave until he was done talking.

He walked around, taking the white light bulbs out of their sockets, replacing them with red ones, then proceeded to sit at the head of the table, with all eyes on him. "The reason I called this meeting is because it's war time. Now I told all of you that before we made that major move we'd have to knock off a few rivals. I stand by that, and now is when we do that." He stood up and looked around the room. Every last one of you muthafuckas in here got my blood in you, and I handpicked you personally to be a part of my dynasty. I put my blood, sweat, and tears in this shit, and now I'm ready to see all of us flourish. But before we begin this process I want y'all to know that I love y'all, but to a certain extent." Wiping his mouth with his hand, he continued to talk, as he was walking around the room.

"I love y'all enough to make y'all rich, to kill for y'all, to trust y'all to handle y'all business as y'all are told to do, but I will not hesitate to take your life." He curled up his lip. "You see, I plan on making y'all the men that I want you all to be, and therefore I have designed a plan for each and every one of you and a certain level of respect, but I will not tolerate any disrespect, shadiness, or cut-throat mentalities. That shit will get you killed quick, and not just you, your newborns, baby mommas, mommas, your whole fucking blood line that stems from you. I will not hesitate to pull your card."

I surveyed the entire room to see the effect he had on everybody and it was mind blowing. Niggas looked at him as if he were God or something. They were in total submission to him, with fear in their eyes. At least that's what I interpreted. The only thing that went through my head was that this man was out of his mind. You see, I never feared my father. I always felt like he had a small man complex and a bad temper. He also had pride issues. I knew he was off of his rocker, but to a certain extent, I mean weren't we all.

All his speech told me was that I always had to remain a few paces ahead of him. I wanted to get the money that he had projected we'd eventually get, my whole life, but I didn't want to run under a loose cannon. I was a born boss, and I had a major problem with authority figures, especially when they were the kind of authority that beat my mother. I felt no kind of love for none of them fools in the room because they reminded me of pimped women. This fool was their mental manipulator, and they looked at him as god. I would never submit to no man the way they were.

"We're going to be taking down Jerry Walker's regime, because we need their territory, and we need him out of the mix. He has too many connections and monopolies around this town that will prevent us from eating the way we are supposed to." He lit a cigarette and inhaled. "So, for the next two weeks our sole mission is to make them niggas miserable. I got vests for everybody, so as long as you don't catch one in the head, I'll be throwing a feast to celebrate our newfound victories. Let's cause hell and show these muthafuckas how Chicago really get down."

That night my father had to take a trip to Mississippi, and before he departed, he made sure to remind my mother of her fate if she tried to test him in any way. He didn't do enough to cause any real damage, but he had to exercise his authority by letting it be known, who ran our household.

Once I heard his car pull away, I crept down to her bedroom and knocked on the door. Through the door, I could make out the painful sobs that occupied her room, anxious to hold her, I turned the knob, letting myself in, closing the door behind me.

She was laying on the bed on her side, adorned in a short night gown, balled into a fetal position. Seeing the confirmation of tears flow down her cheeks, provoked my own, feeling like pins and needles cascading down my cheeks.

I was tired of her getting abused, but more so I was tired of sitting around letting it happen without taking any course of action. I never attempted to do anything because my father had succeeded in instilling fear within us all, so as his children, *we* knew, not to try him.

It ate away at me on a daily basis, and all I could think about was killing this stud, father or not. I slid into her bed and pulled her on top of me. Kissing her lips, I rubbed her back, and held her tightly. "It's okay, momma, I promise you things are going to get better."

Laying her head on my chest, she rubbed my stomach. "I'm tired of being here, son. I can't take it much longer."

I felt her tears drop on to my stomach. My own tears were streaming down my cheeks, saturating my neck. I didn't know what to say to her because she'd been going through the abuse for so long. I felt that she was at a point where words could not help her.

"I'm ready to die, son. I'm ready to leave this earth because it is too painful down here for me, and I can't handle it any longer." She kissed my shoulder. "Between you and your brothers, I feel like you're the only one that genuinely loves me, so tell me, what am I to do?" she asked, straddling me, staring down into my face.

I didn't know what to tell her, but hearing her speak those words broke my heart in half. Envisioning my mother killing herself or harming herself in any way, damn near caused me to have a panic attack. My mother was my strength and my weakness. I didn't think I could go on in life if she was not there. One of the reasons that I had not moved out of the house at that time was because I constantly worried about her, and I needed to be there for her.

"Momma, you are way too strong to be thinking about dying. You are my Queen, and I need you more than anybody on this earth. I don't care about anybody more than you, not even myself. I need you just to be able to make it in this life. If you aren't here, then I have no purpose in breathing."

She groaned, blinked tears and kissed my lips again, just like she used to when I was a little boy. "I love you so much, baby. I need you to rescue me and get me away from here because I want to be there for you, and I need you to be there for me. You're all I have. All of your siblings care about him more than they do me. You're the only one that loves me in this world. "

I pulled her down on top of me and wrapped my arms around the small of her back. After kissing her forehead, and rubbing her soft cheeks for a little while. I promised her that I would find a way to rescue her. That I needed her to be strong for just a short while longer. She agreed, and that night all she wanted was for me to hold her and make her feel protected.

The next day Juice woke me up with two pistols in his hand. He had his shirt off, and a big blunt in his mouth. "Nigga, you ready to go shoot up some dred heads?"

I jumped out of bed and stretched. I didn't know what this fool had in mind, but I had to be down with it because I knew that nine times out of ten my father had already told him what to do and if I didn't follow through word would get back to my old man, and that would make shit tight for me. I had to find a way to get my mother out of his grips, while at the same time capitalizing off his power and prestige.

An hour later, me and Juice were rolling around Memphis smoking a blunt.

"Pops told me to hit them old niggas up where they play chess at the park, and I intend on bodying as many of them as possible." He rubbed his nose, sniffing loudly. "I gotta treat my shit, too. I need some of that raw, so I'mma whip over here and pick up Pac Man. I know bro got that girly on him, and plus he stabbing out wit us. He gon' be a part of my branch of this army."

Pac Man was my brother's best friend. Ever since we came to Memphis, him and Juice had been thick as thieves. Every time Juice got locked up, so did Pac Man. When Pac Man got in some beef, so did my brother. I personally didn't like Pac Man, because I was jealous of him and my brother's relationship. I felt like Juice chose him over me, so I ain't like the nigga one way or the other.

Juice dropped the top on his '64 Chevy Impala. It was all red, with the peanut butter guts, and gold Denaro rims. As soon as he dropped the top, the sun got to tearing my head up. I got hot as hell, and a little irritated.

"Nigga, you fucking Shaneeta daughter yet?"

That question caught me off guard. "What?"

Juice laughed out loud. "Shakia, is you fucking that l'il bitch yet? I peeped how you been spending all this time with her, and I can only imagine that it's because you trying to hit that pussy. So, tell me what's good?"

I knew I had to be feeling something for her because when he called her a bitch I wanted to say something to him about watchin' his mouth, and I ain't never thought about responding like that to him over no other female.

My brother called every female a bitch, even those in our family. I think because he grew up in a household where none of the women were respected and the Queen of our castle was degraded so much that it caused him to just not have that respect for women. I decided to take a cooler approach. I wasn't dumb enough to broadcast my business to him. Hell, we didn't have that type of relationship, being that my father promoted hatred between us.

"Bro, me and Shakia good, she ain't like the rest of these females out here. I got a lot of respect for her."

That sun was baking my face. That was one thing I hated about driving around in a drop top, because if it was too hot, you couldn't really enjoy cruising without the sun whooping your ass. I preferred the air conditioner. To me, fresh air was overrated it if meant that you had to battle all those irritating elements.

My brother kept giving me a crazy look. A look that said that I was full of shit, and he knew it. "Taurus, you must think I'm stupid or something. I know you gotta be fucking her already because shorty ain't even all that. I done seen you bag way badder bitches, so you gotta be on something with her. I just don't know what it is, but I'll tell you what, if you don't fuck her soon, I am."

He pulled up in front of Pac Man's rowhouse. "She been around us way too long for none of us to have hit that pussy yet, that's almost an insult."

I wanted to let bro have it, but I couldn't expose my true emotions for her like that yet. My father had brought us up in a way that said we had to shield our emotions and that we weren't supposed to love anything or anybody. Had I told my brother that I actually cared about Shakia, he would have made it his business to destroy us in one way or another.

My brother didn't like seeing people happy at all, it didn't matter that I was his brother. His whole thing was that if I was to be happy then it meant that I was turning soft, and that wasn't allowed. More of my father had spilled over into him than any one of my siblings.

When he pulled up on Pac Man he was arguing on his phone. There were about twelve grimy looking dudes standing in front of his building drinking forty-ounce beers, and smoking a blunt. I had not seen nobody drinking forty ounces in so long that it shocked me. They eyed us sitting in my brother's whip and gave us a look that said that bet not ever see us over there without Pac Man being present. These dudes looked like they would rob their own mother. Their clothes were dirty, and the few that had hair had nappy braids that looked like they'd been left in for months. Their shoes looked brand new though. The way they looked at us gave me an eerie feeling. I felt like they saw us as prey.

Pac Man Walked over to the '64 and jumped into the back.

"What's good, Juice?" he said shaking up with him. They had their own special handshake. Afterward, he greeted me.

We pulled away from the curb and I noted that all of those

dudes kept looking at us until we disappeared out of their line of vision.

"Yo, Pac Man, who was those dudes that were standing outside of your building?" I needed to know because I felt like one day they would be a problem. Them niggas made me feel some type of way, and if we were going to be going over and picking up Pac Man on a regular basis then I needed to know who we were dealing with.

Pac Man waved them off. "Those are my cousins, kid. They from Haiti, and them niggas crazy as a muthafucka. I don't really rock wit them like that, but it's good though." He tapped my brother on the shoulder and he handed him the blunt. "I'm trying to get my mother to let my l'il sister move down here. She just turned 18, and they ain't treating her right out there in New Jersey."

"Nigga, fuck all of that, what we finna do about these Jerry Walker boys? My old man gave the order to body as many of them niggas as possible, and that's what I plan on doing."

Pac Man lifted his shirt. "I got two .44 Desert Eagles with extended clips. That's 80 rounds. I'm pretty sure I can put at least 60 of these rounds in a few niggaz ass." He took a strong pull from the blunt and handed it to me.

My brother parked the whip, and had his pinkie finger dipping in a bag of pure cocaine treating his nose. He'd snort it up hard, cough, and do it all over again. Pac Man was even worse.

Him and them niggaz down in Black Haven had this thing where they took heroin and put it in a Visine bottle mixed with water. They would shake the bottle up, and snort the drips all day long. They called it dripping. I was in a car with two niggas, and both of them was high as hell. That shit had me put off because it meant that I had to be the designated level head throughout this hit.

We sat there for about an hour, and it felt like it gotten ten times hotter. Out of nowhere I got to sweating like crazy. I ain't like when my clothes stuck to me. That made me overly irritated. It didn't help that my brother had leather seats in his whip. So not only was my back hot as hell, but my ass felt just the same. "Bro, why don't you put this top up? I know you want muhfuckas to see you riding clean and shit, but I'm getting baked like chicken right now."

I could see the sweat all on his forehead. The edges around his dreds were curly as hell, which meant that they were wet.

He looked a little irritated too. "Yeah, you right l'il bro." He started raising the top. "We ain't finna be in this car for a minute anyway."

Pac Man pulled out a big ass screw driver. "I'll be back in five minutes, I'm about to go snatch us up a whip so we can do this move in." About ten minutes later he was back rolling a Buick Skylark.

We sat at the curb around the corner from one of Jerry Walker's gamble houses. It was also known to be an afterhours spot where he'd sell liquor to the hood after the liquor store closed for the night. He'd add a few extra dollars to the original cost of the product, and if you wanted to get drunk bad enough in the wee hours of the night then you'd pay that bill, and most did. This was just one of his places. He had them all around town. My brother decided we'd hit this one because we were sure to come up with a nice amount of paper, and we could get a nice body count to make a statement.

Before this night I had never killed anybody in cold blood, and I wasn't sure if I was ready to do so, but I really didn't have a choice. We were already there and putting on our Barack Obama masks, and black leather gloves. Now I know that most wouldn't pull a caper like this one while there was still light outside, but we were told to make a statement.

We parked the car at the end of the alley, and jogged down it until we got to the garage behind the spot. Once there, we gathered ourselves. I kept the Mach .90 on the side of me. I had 80 shots in the magazine, and another one in my pocket. I was prepared to do some damage, but I was also looking forward to following my brother's lead, because I wasn't sure if I was ready for all of that carnage just yet.

We could hear them in the back-yard shooting dice. It sounded like a bunch of men, and at times they argued, and others, they cracked jokes and laughed loud as hell. I straightened the mask on my face one more time, and cocked my weapon. Pac Man stood up and ran around the side of the garage with Juice right behind him, and me in tow.

"Break yo muthafuckin' self, and don't nobody move!" Pac Man said, before taking one of the Desert Eagles and smacking the shit out of one older dudes with it. He fell straight to the ground holding his mouth.

My brother followed his lead. He smacked one dude with long dreds so hard with the handle of his AK, that it split his head wide open. Pac Man pulled out a pillow case and started dropping all of their money, jewelry, and pistols into it. I was glad that we had got the jump on them because they were strapped with all kinds of guns. Had we chosen to go at them in any other way it would have been a shootout. It blew my mind that they had allowed themselves to be caught off guard.

"Bro, you keep they ass out here, bro you come wit me!" Juice ordered. He ran right up to the back door and kicked it in.

There was a man standing right there on the other side of the door. He'd been getting oral sex from what looked like a dope fiend female. She was real skinny, with a wig that was all twisted on her head. Juice punched her so hard that he knocked her clean out. He turned to the man and popped him three times in his chest. Blood splattered on the steps behind them, and the blasts were so loud that my ears started ringing.

We ran up the steps and into the house, right there in the kitchen there were about four men sitting at the table bagging up crack. When they heard the blast, they went to reach for their weapons, and that was first time I let my Mach bark. I sprayed a dude with some long as dreds who had tried to for a Tech .9 that was on the table. As I saw him going for it, I aimed and pulled the trigger. The bullets spit out in a loud *taat taat taat* sound, ripping apart his neck and jaw. It looked like I was melting allay his face.

Boom! Boom! Boom! I heard Juice's guns as he chopped the other men up that were there. The sight of blood from the first dude that I'd hit got me excited, and I started wetting shit. I was running up on niggas and giving 'em face time. Delivering straight face shots. I loved the way their face would sink in as the bullets ripped into 'em. I got to imagining that these niggas was my father, right after he'd beat my mother. As soon as I saw that image in my head, I went bananas. We left that kitchen looking like a mess.

I followed Juice into the living room, and it was loaded up with all kinds of liquor. It looked like they had just made a major purchase, because it was bottles everywhere, as if they had been waiting to inventory them. There were three other bedrooms in the house and me and Juice took turns kicking in the doors.

The first door I kicked in had an old school nigga with a perm in his head, as soon as the door came in he started firing a revolver with his eyes closed, and thank God for that because the first bullet whipped past my ear stinging it. If he'd had his eyes open he would have knocked my brains out easily. I dropped down to the carpet, and fired my Mach, pumping holes into his chest that looked like I'd hit him with a paintball gun that spit red. He jumped back hard and landed against the wall.

In the other room, I could hear Juice popping his iron back to back. I fucked the room up that I was in, flipping the mattress and finding a kilo of dope. I took a pillowcase and dumped the kilo into it.

Me and Juice met in the living room. He had all kinds of blood splattered across his Obama mask. He grabbed that dope off the table, and ransacked the house coming up with about thirty gees, and we left that muhfucka after leaving the gas on from the stove.

We made it back to our house and disappeared straight to the basement where we split the entire pot. I walked away with fifteen gees, and a kilo of dope that I didn't know the first thing to do with at that time.

That night I had so many nightmares. I dreamed that the two people I killed were coming for my soul. They were asking me why I killed them, crying and chasing me in a cemetery. I woke up eight times that night in a cold sweat. I couldn't go back to sleep.

I got up to go and put some water on my face, and nearly knocked over my mother who was coming out of the bathroom. I still had tears in my eyes and goosebumps all over my skin. As soon as she saw me her eyes got big, and she rubbed my cheek.

"What's the matter, baby?" she whispered, leading me into the bathroom and closing the door behind us.

I couldn't talk. I didn't know what was wrong with me, but I felt sick. I felt like I was about to throw up, and I kept on seeing the faces of the ones I'd killed - the dred headed man and the old school nigga with the perm. "I don't know, momma, but I feel real sick, and cold."

She wrapped her arms around me, and rubbed my back before kissing me on the cheek. "You're okay, baby. Momma is right here, you don't have anything to worry about. I got you. Just tell me what happened."

I wrapped my arms around her and hugged her tightly. I felt her mold into my chest, and instantly I felt better. My mother was my strength in times of weakness. She stood on her tippy toes and kissed my lips twice, before rubbing the back of my neck.

"Tell me, baby." She pressed me forward and I wound up with my back to the wall with her laying her head on my chest.

"I bodied a couple of kats today, and it's eating at my soul, Momma, and I'm just having a hard time dealing with it." I held her tighter.

She groaned. "It's okay, baby. It was bound to happen. That's just the way our family is set up. I know you didn't have a choice." She looked at me with love and understanding. She rubbed my chest and then my stomach. Her touch has always soothed me. I closed my eyes for a moment and let her comfort me. "You see, we don't have a normal family, son. There are going to be some things that you go through in this family that nobody in any other family will ever have to. But you must be strong and just accept it for what it is. It's not your fault." She rubbed my cheek and looked into my eyes with such love. Again, I found myself thinking what a fool my father was. He had a precious gem in her and couldn't even see it. "You're my little baby, and you belong to me. You will always be my little man." She pressed her lips against mine, sucking on them for a bit. "You can never do any wrong in my eyes, son. To me you will always be pure."

My mother's words always made me feel stronger, and so did her kisses. Ever since I could remember, she had always had that healing effect on me. Nobody could heal me the way she could. I loved my mother with all my heart and soul.

"You know what, Momma? The only way I was able to body them niggas was by imagining they were Pops, and he had just got done putting his hands on you. When those images popped into my head, I was able to pull that trigger again and again." I paused and brushed her curly hair away from her face. "I think I'm gon' wind up killing him one day over you."

She looked up at me and blinked tears, before biting into her bottom lip. She shook her head. "All my life, Taurus, I never had nobody stand up for me, or say the things to me that you do. You're messing my head up, baby, because I'm starting to look at you like you're not my son. You make me feel so safe and secure. I feel like a little girl around you instead of your mother, and I don't know how to handle those feelings. What am I supposed to do?" She looked deep into my eyes.

I could tell that she expected me to have it all figured out, but I didn't. I didn't even know what to say. I just held her tighter, and kissed her forehead.

Chapter 7

We'd made so much of a splash against Jerry Walker and his crew that he sent a message to my father saying he wanted to have a sit down to discuss business in the south. My father said that he wanted to have Juice with him along with his regular security detail which included Pac Man. They were to have the sit down out in Houston, Texas. Although my father said I could not be present in the board room, he ordered that I rollout to the city, so me and Tywain caught a flight the day before they did.

Tywain had a female cousin by the name of Blaze that was so fine, I couldn't take my eyes off her. She was just 21 years old, and worked as a stripper. She was brown skinned, with dimples on both of her cheeks like me. Her hair was cut into a short curly style, and shaved on the sides. Her body was so cold. She was thick as a muthafucka, with no stomach.

She pulled up in front of the airport in a drop top pink Lexus, with the hot pink rims that matched her car. The interior of her whip was all white Louis Vuitton. Blaze stepped out of the whip and ran up to Tywain, and I noted that she rocked a Louis Vuitton business suit that hugged her so right that I wanted to shoot my shot right then and there. I already sized her up and figured that she would be one of those stuck up chicks who thought the world belonged to them.

I ain't really mind her thinking that the world belonged to her, but the stuck-up thing would get on my nerves. Imagine how I felt when after she hugged Tywain she walked right over to me and wrapped her arms around me.

"You must be Taurus, damn Playboy, you got all them muscles and thangs, I bet you a snatch my l'il ass up, huh?" I embraced her and she smelled so damn good. Not only was she fine as hell, but she had the swag, and the scent to match her essence.

I kissed her on the neck, not giving a fuck what that nigga Tywain was gon' say. "Damn shorty, you smell good as hell. I hope you can get rid of yo nigga while I'm down here, because I gotta see what this be like." I trailed my hands down and rubbed them all over that big ass ghetto booty. When it came to these broads in the streets, I had to play the role. Every chick out here wanted a hood nigga.

She ain't say nothing, just let me do me until I finished by cupping it. She turned to Tywain. "I like him, Tywain. I see why you always hollering his name." She kissed me on the cheek. "Don't worry about it, baby, we both grown."

We hopped in her whip and rolled around the big city for about an hour before pulling up to Blaze's house. From the outside, it looked like a normal two story suburban house. It was painted gray and steel blue. I nodded my head. I mean she was only 21, so for her to have her own house already was a little fascinating to me.

"Say, Blaze, you own this house right here?"

She closed her car door and put her Louis Vuitton bag over her shoulder. "Yeah, my old man left it to me when he passed away. It ain't much, but I'm thankful for it." She adjusted the bag on her shoulder. "Y'all come on, I got a bunch of people I want ya'll to meet."

Instead of us going on to the porch to enter the house, we followed her around the side through a wooden picket fence. Walking closer to the fence, I could hear laughing and the splashing of water.

She opened the door and it was like I had died and gone to Heaven. I had to pause in my tracks just to take in the sights of the backyard. Everywhere I looked, there was a female dressed in a bikini so small that the material was basically pointless. I saw a lot of different races and mixtures, too. The two Asian and Black chicks were strapped. They had to be sisters because they looked just a like. Their asses were so big, my mans below instantly went on brick. Then the l'il gathering had a few chocolate sisters that made me forget about the Asian and Black chicks almost immediately. The way the sun made their dark skin pop had me feeling some type of way, and they were just as thick. The red bones were peppered in too, and they weren't short stopping either. I stood there frozen by the entrance, for a full minute with my mouth hanging wide open.

After we got in and Blaze introduced us to everybody, I found out that most of the girls worked at her club, and they were top-notch money earners. I could see why. I could have got a lap dance from every one of them in the same night. I ain't playing either.

We kicked it around the big above ground pool for about We kicked it around the big above ground pool for about three hours. I didn't get in the water, but Tywain did. When the girls found out that he was her cousin they started to show him mad love. They were all over him. Every time they started to show me any kind of attention, Blaze interrupted the conversation and pulled me away. I could tell she had a thing for me.

The last time it happened, it was about 1 in the morning, and the Asian and Black sisters had me trapped in the hallway of Blaze's house and feeling all over my chest and abs. I think they were getting ready to flip my ass, when Blaze bent the corner and broke it up.

"Y'all better get away from him. I told y'all that this Chicago nigga is mine. I been wanting to see how they get down out there." She pulled me by the arm toward the kitchen. "Y'all can fuck with my cousin. Show him what it do." I watched her ass jiggle in her little boy shorts as she escorted me into the kitchen.

She bent over and grabbed a bottle of Ace of Spades out of the refrigerator before closing it back. Still holding my hand, she led me into the living room and she knelt in front of the fireplace.

She popped the cork out of the bottle, and the fizz spilled over her hand. She licked the juices up and smiled at me. "I like you, Taurus. You a fine city boy, ain't you?"

I already had my shirt off, and because me and the homey ain't have no swim trunks I was walking around in my boxers. She had on a little wife beater, and the smallest pair of pink Victoria Secrets boy shorts. They were all up in her ass and in her crotch. When she squatted down, the shorts split her crease and I saw both naked pussy lips come out on each side. I grabbed my pipe immediately because I knew I was about to pitch a tent.

"You ever see a real bad bitch twerk before?" she asked, getting on all fours after setting the bottle of Ace to the side. She clapped her hands and her sound system came on as if on que. She slowly wiggled her ass in a circle, looking back at me over her shoulder. Then she pulled the shorts so that they exposed the outline of her pussy, after that she popped her ass hard, making it jiggle. It looked so good to me. When she closed her eyes, and ran her fingers between her legs, separating her lips, I found myself on my knees behind her kissing all up and down that pussy. I had my nose in her ass and everything and I didn't even care. She pulled her leg band all the way to the side so that her pussy was out. I slurped it into my mouth like it was oysters or something. She moaned real deep in her throat, reached back and separated her ass cheeks.

"Fuck that tongue, I want you to fuck me with that big ass Chicago dick! Take my pussy, now!"

That was all she had to say. I tackled her ass to the carpet, stuck my forearm in the small of her back, and ripped her boy shorts right off of her while she moaned. I mean I ripped them muhfuckas off like I was raping her for real, and in my mind, I probably was. Once they cleared her body, I pulled her up and made her stick her face in the carpet, took my dick and shoved it into her fat ass pussy and started fucking her so hard that it hurt my stomach. I was long stroking that pussy, and her juices were squirting out of her.

The way she screamed and moaned was giving me motivation to maintain my assault. It ended with me forcing her into a ball while I plunged into her pussy again and again. It was crazy because Tywain sat right on the side of me downing the two sisters one after the other. We spent all night screwing, and by the time the sun came up the next day I was exhausted and hungry as hell.

The next day we met up with my brother, Juice, before him and my father went to the business meeting with Jerry Walker. He looked like he was ready for action. He'd rented a Lexus truck, and as I sat in the passenger's seat the A.C. felt cool on my face.

"L'il brother, no matter what go down wit Pops today I'm letting you know now that when we get back to Memphis we about to break out and make shit happen for ourselves. We got more than enough work to hit the ground running for ourselves." He lit a Black and Mild, and cracked his window. A part of me knew that what he was saying was true, but something in me knew not to trust him. Most of his life, he walked in our father's shadow.

Why did he wanna do things differently, all of a sudden?

Tywain sparked a blunt in the back seat and passed it to me before lighting two more and passing one to my brother and keeping one for his self. Smoke invaded the car in thick clouds. It didn't take long before I was high as the Statue of Liberty's torch.

"Bro, you already know I'm down for whatever. So, however you wanna move, just let me know, and me and the Homey gon' be right there in motion." I still had a whole kilo of dope ducked off that he didn't know about. My plan was to pop that and get my chips up so I could hide my mother from my old man. I just wasn't sure where I was gone have her travel away to yet.

"Long as you niggas don't forget about the kid," Tywain said, sipping on some Lean. "I got a whole apartment complex that my doped-up uncle own we can hustle out of over in White Head. That nigga a slumlord anyway. All we gotta do is hit him with a little bit of nothing and he'll give us a few of the apartments to do our thing out of." Tywain hit his blunt and inhaled it loudly.

"You already know we ain't gone forget about you, L'il bro. You're family in my eyes." Juice reassured him before turning into a pizza joint where the waitresses rolled around on skates.

A nice Mexican-looking female with some thick thighs rolled over to his Lexus truck with a menu in her hand. "May I take your order?" She had long silky black hair and a round pretty face.

Juice rolled down the window and blew a cloud of smoke into her face. She closed her eyes and frowned. He laughed. "Damn, mami, what, you afraid of the Ganja?" That was just like his ass to be picking on people for no reason. He was a bully just like our father.

She fanned her face. "No, it's not that. I just can't go back to work smelling like drugs. They'll try to fire me like they did my co-worker, Melissa." She fanned her face again and dusted off clothes. "I need this job."

Juice leaned out of the window. "That's my bad, baby girl. The last thing I'd want for you to do is lose your job." He looked past her shoulder and out to the establishment. "Say, whatchu making working here?"

She shrugged her shoulders. "Just minimum wage, but in a year, I should move up a few dollars." She looked like she was turning sad. I guessed that hearing her situation out loud was affecting her in some type of way.

Juice laughed. "You mean to tell me that you're rolling around on skates for these muhfuckas and they only paying you minimum wage? Nah, fuck that. Why don't you quit and come work for me?"

She gave him a look that said he must have been out of his

mind. "I don't even know you."

"So, what. You didn't know them either and you walked up to their establishment and asked for a job. So why can't I offer you one?"

She paused, and bit into her lower lip, adjusting her weight from one foot to the other owe. "What would you hire me to do?"

He laughed. "I think you should be more worried about how much I'm willing to pay you. A female as fine as you shouldn't be working in a place like this. You look like a classy chick." After saying this he reached out and rubbed her chin.

She smiled lightly, and lowered her head as if she were shy or something. I could tell that the game my brother was spitting to her was influencing her by the way she let her guards down.

When she first rolled over to us, she stood a safe distance away from the truck. Now, she had moved so close to the truck that he was able to put his arm out of the window. I could tell he was rubbing her ass.

"Well, I just moved up here from Mexico, and I'm trying to figure life out. If you think you have a better game plan for me than this I'm all ears." She leaned into the window and I could smell her perfume. I wasn't impressed by the scent.

Juice opened the door to his truck and got out. He put his arm around her shoulders and got to whispering in her ear. After that conversation, she would become his face; meaning she would be the chick he got to get under dudes with a lot of money and once they started to feel something for her she would go in for the kill. My brother eventually hit many of his licks by using her.

That night my father had his meeting with Jerry Walker and I was told by Juice that they had come to some form of an understanding that worked out for both ends. My father was finally to get his piece of the pie, and all it took was a little bloodshed to make it happen.

Back at Blaze's house, me and Tywain made plots of our

own. I told him about the kilo of dope that I had put up, and that I wanted to do something special for somebody in my life with some of the proceeds.

Tywain didn't care. The only thing that was on his mind was the fact that I had a kilo of dope, and it was all pure powder. "Yo, we can get my aunt to chef that shit up for us. We can triple our money. She a beast at that shit too," he said, adding a four to his Sprite turning it pink.

I didn't fuck with that Lean shit. I'd tried it one time and all it did was make me sleepy. I couldn't function under those conditions. I needed to be alert and I never understood why other niggas liked that shit. How could you be in the streets sleepy?

"You know I'm new to the game, bro, but I catch on real fast. If your aunt gone make sure we straight, then out of the 36 zips nigga half is yours. I wanna see you eat just like me."

Blaze came into the den wearing a Prada blue swim suit. She looked like a goddess. She motioned with her fingers for me to walk over to her, so I got up. "Yo, Tywain, me and you will talk business later. I'm about to go and see what she want."

When we were out of the den, she wrapped her arms around my neck and licked my lips before sucking on them hard. She couldn't have been more than five feet two inches tall, so she had to stand on her tippy toes. I thought it was so sexy when short females did that. I loved women shorter than me, and being that I was 6 feet 2, that was almost all women, but I had a special thing for those 5 feet 5 and shorter.

"I want you to stay here in Texas, Taurus, so I take care of you. I'll put you all the way on your feet. Or fuck it, you ain't gotta work at all. I just love your swag, and I wanna see you having chips."

She kissed my lips again and reached between us grabbing my dick. "These niggaz scared to fuck me the way that you do. They look at my pretty face and thick body, and most of them niggaz can't even perform. But you can! You fucked me so good that I'm ready to empty out my bank account right now and give all of that shit to you, because I know I can get it back if you're by my side." She kissed my neck and bit into it. "I eavesdropped on y'all conversation a little bit and I heard you saying that you got a kilo, so I'm guessing that it means you're in the game. What if I told you that I got connects down south of the border that will put you all the way in? What would you say to that?" She stuck her hand under my Polo shirt and rubbed my abs.

All I could hear was the money sound of ca-CHING! I was willing to do whatever it took to come up with that plug. I didn't know who she knew, or how deep they were plugged into the game, but she didn't strike me as the type that wasn't about her paper on all levels. I just had to see what angle she was coming from.

"Who is this plug, and how you know they gon' fuck wit me?"

She waved me off. "Nall, you don't worry about that because they gone fuck wit me, and I'm gone fuck wit you, as long as you're my man." She turned her head to the side in a sexy way.

I pulled her into my warm embrace. "I don't know about up-rooting and moving out here to Houston right away, but what I will tell you is that it's definitely on the table."

I could feel her become excited. "That's what's good. I'll tell you what. I'm about to be touring all over the States for about 4 months. After then why don't me and you link up to see what's good? That sound like a plan to you?"

Not only did it sound like a plan to me, but four months would give me enough time to try and get my weight up on my own. If at the end of that time I was not where I wanted to be, I could always fall back on her. "That sounds good, shorty. You just do everything that you need to do and in a few months, we'll link up."

She gave me a look that said she was a little hurt. "You mean to tell me that you can stay away from me for that long?" She looked offended, poking her lip out resembling a little kid that was pouting. "So, what am I supposed to do when I need this pussy beat in the right way?"

I wrapped her back in my arms, and ran my hands down to that plump ass booty, after squeezing it, I sucked on her neck.

"Anytime you're in Memphis all you gotta do is hit me up, or if need be I'll travel to wherever you send me a ticket to fly to."

She dropped down to her knees, and pulled out my dick. "Ah so as long as I'm footing the bill you'll come whenever I send for you?"

I nodded and slid into her mouth. "Like clockwork."

Chapter 8

We had been back in Memphis for only two weeks when the Feds kicked in the door to our house at three in the morning and snatched up my old man. I'll never forget that night because earlier that day we had met around the table in the basement to discuss how my father was going to execute his plans. He didn't say much about the Jerry Walker meeting. I told myself that I would squeeze the information about the meeting from Juice later. That was before I found out that Juice had not been directly inside of the room where my father and Jerry Walker had their sit down. I guess they had agreed that no one other than them would be allowed inside. The only things my father spoke about that evening was how we were supposed to coincide with Jerry's men. He also explained our new territories and what belonged to Jerry Walker.

The meeting was boring, and I didn't get a full understanding as to when everything was to take place. My father basically said that after all the logistics were figured out that he'd let us know.

Coming from out of the basement, I was stuck in a state of confusion. One thing that always helped me to get my mind in order was a nice quiet drive through the city. That's what I figured I'd do. As I made my way to my whip, it was just starting to rain really hard. So, I jogged to the car, and after struggling to get the key in the lock, I heard Shakia calling me. I got into the car and waved her over. She ran over with an umbrella over her head. I popped the lock on the passenger's door and she got in.

"Dang, I thought you was finna act like you couldn't hear me or something." She fixed the umbrella so she could put it away. "Where you about to go? And why you ain't return my phone call like you told me you would last night?" She looked my way, waiting for me to give her a response.

I threw the car in drive and pulled out into the street, without saying, nor answering her question. After cruising for a little while, I turned on some Aaliyah. One thing about Aaliyah, her voice always took me to a calm and soothing place in my mind. I was trying to figure out what I was going to say to her because ever since I came back from Texas, I just felt weird facing her. I think it was that I respected her so much that it was hard to face her because what had taken place between me and Blaze. I felt like I had betrayed her in some way and those were new emotions for me that I didn't quite understand, because I'd never given a fuck about cheating on a female. In fact, I never considered it cheating because I told them what it was upfront. I took a deep breath and turned to her.

"You wanna blow some Loud wit me?" I knew she really didn't smoke weed a lot, but she would at times with me.

She lowered her head. "That must mean you got something real bad to tell me, huh?" She put her seatbelt around her, sat back, and crossed her arms over her chest.

I turned my windshield wipers on high because the rain was really coming down. I could barely see out. I decided to pull into a Taco restaurant parking lot. After parking I turned the ignition off but kept the music playing. "Why you think I got something bad to tell you?" I took a blunt out of my glove box and set fire to it.

"Because, you've been acting real funny toward me ever since you got back from Texas. Not only that, I miss the way you used to treat me like I was special. Like you'd always come over and check in on me before you called it a night. Then, you'd at least return my texts. For a few weeks now you haven't even done that. So, what gives?"

I handed her the blunt and watched as she took two small puffs before passing it back to me. I did have a crazy thing for her, and as she sat there in my presence a whole slew of emotions starting to explode inside of me. "I'm just gone keep shit real. I fucked another broad while I was down there. A l'il chick named Blaze. She my nigga cousin. The reason why I've been so distant is because I didn't know how to face you. I feel like I betrayed you in some way, and that's eating at me. "

I was already feeling the high, and for some reason I didn't even feel like finishing the blunt. I handed it to her and she held it for a brief moment, then sat it in the ashtray.

"I figured that you had did something, but I don't think that's a reason for you to punish me." She looked out of her window and shook her head. "I mean, if you won't protect me then who will, Taurus? My whole life that is all that I've ever wanted was for a boy to like me enough to protect me, and be faithful to me. I'm starting to think that that's just wishful thinking." She exhaled and sat in silence.

I really didn't know what to say to her, because I knew that I had hurt her feelings. I cared about Shakia, and I wanted her to be my woman, but I didn't think I had that whole faithful bone in my body. I loved pussy, and the first thing that came to my mind when I saw a bad chick was I wondered what her pussy felt like, and how she got down in that bedroom. I couldn't help that for the life of me. "Look, Shakia, I care about you and you know that I will never allow nobody to hurt you."

"Taurus, damn everybody else, you're hurting me!" she whimpered. "I told you in the beginning what I expected from you, and you said that you still wanted me to be your girl. You could have continued to let us be friends. Why would you play with my heart this way?" She opened the car door and ran out of it.

Shit! "Shakia!" I got out of the car and ran behind her. The rain felt like pellets hitting me all over my body. My clothes were drenched in a matter of minutes, and the longer I ran the heavier they became. Shakia was running so fast that for a minute I thought that I would not be able to catch her, until finally she stopped in somebody's backyard and sat on their porch with her hand covering her face. "It's not fair, Taurus. It's not fair! You're supposed to protect me, and be there for me no matter what. You're not supposed to choose another female over me just because I'm not in your presence for a few days. Do you have any idea what that does to my self-esteem? I mean how are you so different from Greg?"

I heard the thunder roar overhead and a part of me got spooked. I didn't mess with Mother Nature like that, and I feared getting struck down by lightning. I knew that I owed her an explanation for things, and I felt horrible about the way she was feeling, but I didn't want to have the conversation outside, at least not at that time. "Shakia, baby, let's talk about this in the car, girl, before we get struck by lightning."

She put her face in her arms and cried harder. "That's what you have to say to me. You wanna talk about the fucking weather and I'm sitting over here with a broken heart and I don't even know what to do with myself right now. I fucking love you, Taurus, and you don't even care." She stood up like she was preparing to run again, but I reached out and grabbed her arm. "Let me go!"

The lightning struck a tree in the next yard, knocking it over. I felt chills travel down my spine, and the wind picked up speed, damn near knocking us over. I pulled her closer to me, and put my lips to her ear. The tension left her body as she melted into my arms. "I love you, girl. You have to know that. But I'm not ready to leave them streets alone. I want you to be my number one, but that's all I can offer right now. Now you gotta respect that."

The wind picked up to the point I was fearing a Tornado coming. It was taking all the strength I had to stand up, and the harder the wind blew it made the rain feel like hail. Thunder roared, and once again the lightning struck close by. It sounded like a shotgun blast.

"Your number one!" She struggled to stay on her feet. "What does that even mean?" She wrapped her arms around me and tried to keep her balance.

The wind started to blow harder. It picked up its strength along with the rain. The sky got completely dark, and I could not see in front of me anymore. "Look, Shakia, let's run back to the car and we can finish this conversation there. Okay!"

She screamed, "Okay!"

We took off running with me holding her hand. It was so far to travel. It felt like the wind was trying to knock us over at every stride. Lightning struck a tree right in front of us. The tree fell on to a power line and sparks shot across the street. We ran faster and barely made it to my car when the wind got so strong that it felt like we were being pulled. As soon as we were both in the car, I started it and stepped on to the gas after turning my windshield wipers on.

"Oh, my God!" Shakia screamed.

I looked in my rearview mirror to see that there was a Tornado forming behind us. That freaked me out. I pressed down on the gas a little harder, speeding away from danger. The only thing on my mind was getting us to safety.

We listened to the radio as they spoke about a Tornado in our area. I got on to the express way and we wound up on the east side of town where it was safe. I got to worrying about my mother, but we live chatted and she appeared to be okay.

Her and the rest of the family were in the basement hoping that the storm would past. After I finished checking in with her, I pulled into the Radisson, where me and Shakia got a room. We immediately changed out of our wet articles of clothing, into something more warm and comfortable.

"I'm so sorry, Taurus. Please forgive me," she said, walking up to me and wrapping her arms around my waist, her head pressed to my chest.

"Why are you apologizing?" I asked, still trying to figure out how we were going to finish our discussion. "I'm the one that was in the wrong."

She broke the embrace and started to pace the floor. "It's not really your fault. I knew I wasn't supposed to put that pressure on you like that. Ever since I've known you you've had a lot of females. Why should I expect that to change just because I'm in the picture now?" She shook her head. "Then I'm so freaking emotional over you. I can't handle myself, and I think it's because I've had a crush on you for so long, that now that I have you I can't control myself."

I got up and blocked her path. "Chill, right now you're just over thinking everything." I hugged her. "I was in the wrong for stepping out on you when we had the understanding that we were going to be monogamous, that's my fault. But that does not mean that I don't care about you, because I do. I love you, Shakia, and that's real. I just got some kind of a sex addiction, and it's hard for me to turn down pussy, but that's not your fault, it's mine."

She shook herself out of my embrace. "You know what? I'm so sick of everything constantly coming back to that. Just fuck me right now, Taurus." She started unraveling the robe that was supplied by the hotel. "I'm serious. Maybe if I started giving the pussy away niggaz would actually wanna stay with my ass."

I stood watching her with my eyes wide open. "Yo, we ain't finna do this like that, Shakia. You're going through something, and you're reading our situation wrong. It's not about that."

She kicked off her Jordans and started to pull her tight capris down exposing pink bikini cut panties. "Don't you tell me that this is not what it's all about. That's all men care about is the pussy. So I want you to take mine, so that way you can stay with me, and you don't have to ride all the way to Texas just to get some. Besides, I'm ready to fuck. I been ready for a long time, and tonight is the night." After dropping her pants, she walked over to me and started to unbuckle my Tom Ford jeans. I looked at the way her titties were jiggled, and I couldn't even lie - I got turned on like a muthafucka. When she bent all the way over I saw a hint of her brown areolas, causing my dick to rise to the occasion. She squeezed it through my pants.

Every part of me wanted to stop her because I knew she was acting off of hurt emotions, but like I said before, I was addicted to sex, and I could smell a hint of her essence in the air. Like maybe because we'd been running around outside she was a little sweaty. Whatever the case, that smelled good to me, and I wanted in. When she got my pants down, she pulled by boxers down along with them. "Shakia, you ain't gotta do this, baby, you know that, right?" I felt her hot hand massaging my manhood, and the feeling made my knees buckle. As much as it tore me to see how she truly valued herself, I couldn't help but think with the head below my waistline. I yearned for that warmth.

"I just want my man to fuck me. Is that okay? I mean you are my man, right?" she asked looking up at me licking her lips.

Fuck it! It's not like I haven't wanted her for a long time with her fine ass! I reached down and ripped her bra off exposing her pretty titties. They had big nipples on them that stood at attention, and after I saw them all bets were off. "Hell yeah I'm yo man."

"Okay then," she took my dick into her motuh and sucked on him so hard that I groaned a little bit. I felt her wrap her tongue around the head, before sucking up and down him like she hungered for his juices. She popped him out of her mouth briefly. "Do you like that, baby? Is this gone make me be one of your favorite girls?" She started to suck me like a porn star. I had to lean against the wall while she did her thing.

I got to thinking about all kinds of freaky shit in my head, and I could not get around the fact that I had her on her knees performing for me. First her mother, then her, that shit was definitely hot to me.

I didn't play no games. I snatched her little ass up and pushed her knees to her chest and ate her pussy for almost a full hour. By the time I was done, she had come so much that she couldn't move. She was begging me to fuck her, and I wasted no time. I put her thighs onto my forearms and took my time being that I was her first. She bled at first, confirming that she was a virgin. She had tears in her eyes, and I only stopped for a brief second to take in the fact that her flower was gone.

After the moment passed, I got to dogging that pussy, and she tried to run all over the room. I grabbed her leg, and pull her back to the floor, where I folded her up and beat it some more. The pussy was good. I had to murder it from the back while I smacked them thick ass cheeks. The sounds she made only motivated me to go harder and deeper. I fucked her until my dick wouldn't rise no more.

I sucked them thick nipples while she cried and told me how much she loved me. She said she didn't mind if I had other chicks on the side, just as long as she was my number one. We didn't have any intentions on staying at the hotel, so before we left the room that night, we got a good understanding.

We strolled out at about three in the morning and I was exhausted. Everything on me hurt. I pulled up in front of her house first and she acted like she didn't want to get out of the car.

"Baby, it's good. I promise I'm gone be one hunnit to you. We got an understanding. All you gotta do is play your role, that's it."

She reached over and squeezed my thigh. "But I love you, Taurus, and I don't want you to forget about how much you mean to me. I will literally die without you. I'm not playing either."

I grabbed her by her hair and tongued her down. She moaned into my mouth, and rubbed my abs through my shirt. After we broke the kiss I wiped my lips. "You mine, Shakia, and I got you. Go get some sleep, baby." She kissed me again and got out of the car with tears in her eyes.

She ran all the way to her front door, then turned around and ran back to the car. I rolled down my passenger's window.

She said, "I love you, baby, and I'll see you in the morning. Do you want me to bring you breakfast over?"

I laughed. "Nall, I'm good. All I want you to do is to go and get some rest. I want you to ride with me tomorrow."

She looked like I'd just gave her a million dollars. Her eyes lit up, and she made a squealing sound. "Okay, baby, I'll see you at about 11. I love you."

I told her that I loved her as well, and I did, I just didn't know to what extent.

That night I slept good as hell. It was still raining when I laid down and the rain always, made me go into a deep sleep for some reason. Luckily, the storms had passed and the tornado had not done much damage to our area. Just a few trees and power lines had gone down. I made sure that I opened my window that night before I fell out so I could hear the rain beating against the pavement better.

I couldn't have gotten more than two hours of sleep before I saw a bright light in my dreams. I felt like I was a deer and I had been caught in some headlights, but then I was smacked so hard that I woke up. What I saw was masked faces in all black pointing assault rifles at me. I damn wear shit on myself. I just knew they were going to kill me.

"Don't move! Don't move motherfucker!" They screamed with muffled voices. They were holding flashlights as well as their weapons. I thought that we were being robbed and the first thing that came to my mind was the fact that I had given my kilo to Tywain so that his Aunt could cook it up for us. I was so thankful that our product was not there.

It didn't take long for my conscious mind to kick in before I knew we were being raided by the Feds. That scared me even more because I got to thinking about the niggaz I'd killed. I got to imagining doing life plus in prison, and felt like throwin' up all over the floor, especially when they picked me up and slammed me on my face right next to my mother, who had tears in her eyes. She looked sick. That broke my heart. One of the agents had his feet in her back. I wanted to kill his ass dead. I wished that I could have seen his face.

They ransacked our house, and didn't find anything other than my father. That's who they had been looking for. They snatched him up and left our home in shambles. It looked like we had been hit by a tornado. We were so blessed that they did not take us downtown for questioning, or anything like that. I guessed that it was all about my father. I didn't know what he'd gotten himself into at that time, but later on I'd found out that he was on Federal probation, and was not supposed to have left Chicago or the state of Illinois. They returned him to federal prison where he was made to finish his remaining time of 27 months.

My mother waited until the next day to pull me into her room where she broke down in my arms. "Baby, I don't know what we're going to do. Now that your father is gone. How will we survive? How will these bills get paid? My whole life I've always depended on him, since the tender age of 14. I never had my own when I was with him. Even during the times I worked, he was in control of my money and his, our finances as a whole. I never got to see any of it. Now, what are we gonna do? I'm so scared for us, baby," she cried, squeezing me tighter and tighter.

I held her out in front of me and looked her in the eyes. "Don't you understand that that had to happen in order for our lives to take off the way they're supposed to?" I shook my head. "That man ain't never did nothing but hurt you. Now we got a little breathing room and me finding a way to get you out of here and into a better life will be a little easier. I thought you believed in me?"

She threw her arms around my neck and started to kiss all over my face. "Baby, I do believe in you. And I know you got us. I'm just letting you know that I'm scared, that's all. Please don't be mad at me, because I need you right now." She rubbed the sides of my face with her thumbs before kissing me on the lips and sucking on them roughly. "I believe in you, baby, I always have."

I pulled her closer to me and wrapped my arms all the way around her. She felt molded to my body, and her perfume went right up my nose intoxicating me. She humped her hips forward, and moaned in my ear before sucking on my ear lobe. "It's been so long, baby. So long, and I need you so bad." She whimpered.

I kissed her forehead and took her arms from around me.

"Momma, I love you, and we're gonna get through this. Your l'il man about to make it happen for this family. All I need is for you to believe in me, and not worry about nothing because I got this. You're my baby now. Just let me protect you."

After that night, I made up my mind that I was about to make it happen for my mother first, and then the family. I didn't know what Juice had in mind, but I knew that I would make it happen by any means.

My mother kissed my lips again and pulled me more firmly into her. She looked into my eyes, and bit into her bottom lip.

"I need you, baby. And the way that I need you isn't right. I don't know what to do." She ran her hand under my shirt and over my stomach where she squeezed the muscles. "I need you so damn bad." She moaned and closed her eyes.

I didn't really know how to feel about her in that moment. I guess a part of me was a little confused. I knew who she was to me, and I was having a hard time respecting that fact. My mother was a real beautiful woman, and very affectionate. I had always said to myself that I had never seen any other female that was as bad as her. I was one of those little boys that grew up having a crush on their mother. I don't think I understood that that wasn't appropriate until I was about 12 years old. By that time, I had already fantasized about a lot of things involving her that I don't even speak on. I felt her kissing on my neck, and as if on their own my hands rubbed down her back and cupped her juicy butt cheeks. They felt soft in my hands, and the silk of her gown only added to the feeling.

"Umm yeah, it's okay, baby. Do whatever comes to your mind because I need you so bad. That man ain't touched me in years." She bit into my neck, and licked my ear lobe. I pulled the back of her gown up. She had a mirror that hung on the back of her bedroom door, and I watched myself exposing more and more of her until her bare ass cheeks appeared in the mirror. They were round, and golden, the same color as her skin everywhere else. I felt myself becoming excited as she moaned into my ear and humped into me.

"Please touch me, baby. Your momma needs to be healed. Please, baby, I swear I won't tell nobody. Just do me right, son." She licked my neck, and bit into it, moaning deep within her throat.

Her touches started to get to me. I felt myself getting harder and harder until I picked her up off of the ground. She wrapped her legs around me. I crashed into the wall with her, sucking all over her lips and neck.

"Please do me, baby. Make momma feel loved. I need you right now, sugah."

We fell to the bed with me between her legs. Our tongues wrestled, and our breathing was labored and heavy. I don't know what was running through my mind. I think that since everything was feeling so good I didn't want to make too much of what we were doing. The forbidden aspect of it all excited me some.

My mother had not felt loved in a very long time. I liked the fact that she needed me, and that it was I that she turned to instead of anybody else. She opened her legs wide and her gown rode up, exposing her hairy valley. Her lips were wet, and the hair looked as if they had clear gel all over them. I smelled her scent and it drove me crazy. When she reached down and separated her sex lips, I had made my mind up right there that I wanted to heal her by any means. I leaned down and bit into her thick thigh, and that's when my sister started knocking on her bedroom door.

We scrambled to get dressed. As soon as we were decent enough, my mother opened the door, and I stepped past my sister who ran right into my mother's arms. She was still emotional over my father getting arrested. Before I completely disappeared, I looked over my shoulder one time, and me and my mother made eye contact as she held my sister in her arms. Her look told me that she didn't regret anything, and that she needed me. All I could do was nod my head.

Chapter 9

I linked up with Tywain about an hour later. He pulled up to my house in a Lincoln Town car that I had never seen him in before. I was sitting on the porch trying to make sense of what happened between me and my mother. I wasn't feeling remorseful or anything. I was more or less trying to figure out our situation and how I could really be there for her. I didn't care about what society said. Or what people thought outside of me and her, because they didn't matter. I loved my mother and I would do anything for her. She was the one woman on this earth that went through it all for me and my siblings and for that I could never repay her. So, in any way that I could get as close to repaying her as possible, I was willing to do it with no hesitation. Besides, I ain't want her looking to nobody other than me anyway. I would hold her down one hundred percent.

Tywain caught me thinking about her. He'd manage to get all the way up to the porch before I clicked back into reality.

"Nigga, what's good?" he asked, shaking my hand. "I hope you ready to get this money, because I got some people I want to introduce you to."

As he was saying that Shakia came out of her house and jogged over to me until she wrapped her arms around my neck. I tongued her down while rubbing all over that fat booty.

"Hey baby, I just wanted to catch you before you left the house. Do you know when we'll have time to be alone together?" she asked, eyeing Tywain up and down.

He laughed out loud with his fist covering his mouth. "Damn so now it's like that? What happened to us all kicking it like we used to?" He looked a little hurt. I could tell he was checking out her ass in them all white jogging pants she was wearing. They hugged her so good that I wanted to take her into my bedroom and wear that ass out.

"He's my man now, so I shouldn't have to share him all the time. So whatever y'all about to go and do, do it, and then hopefully me and him will link up later," she said this looking at me from the corners of her eyes. "Right, baby?"

I nodded, laughing. "Yeah, that's cool. I need some time alone with my baby anyway." I pulled her to me and sucked on her neck, before biting that thick ass vein on the side. She moaned in my ear, and I squeezed that booty. "This mine right here, ain't that right baby?"

"Hell yeah."

Tywain curled his lip. "Damn, she done got thick as hell. I see why you snatched her up. It was time. Fuck!" He shook his head as if he couldn't believe she had gotten so bad.

Juice pulled up with three cars following behind him. They all parked and he hopped out of his car without opening the doors. The men followed behind him. They all had red bandanas around their necks and head. He walked up to me and pulled me to the side.

"I'm fucking with the Bloodz now, and we about to do our own thing. I can't sit around and wait for Pops to get out of jail in damn near three years. I'm ready to get money right now and my Blood niggaz gone hold me down. Fuck wit me on half of that kilo that I know you gave Tywain to cook up for you," he said, looking over his shoulder at Tywain.

I shot daggers with my eyes at my homey. "How you know about that?" I asked in irritation. I had plans on flipping that bird on my own. It was enough that I had promised Tywain half. Now my brother was trying to get half, which meant that somebody was gone come up short, and it wasn't gone be me.

Juice snapped his head back like he was offended. "Since when we start keeping secrets?" He called Tywain over and looked him up and down. "What...you wasn't supposed to tell me about that l'il weak ass bird or something?"

Tywain looked at me, and back to Juice. "Fuck you talking about, Juice?" He had a look on his face that said he didn't like how Juice was coming at him. One thing I knew about Tywain was that he didnt bow down to no man. He didn't give a fuck who you were. If he felt like you were coming at him bogus you was finna hear about that.

Juice laughed and ran his hand over his face. He took a deep breath as if he were trying to calm down. "Look, bro, I just asked my l'il brother to hit me wit half of that bird, and he made it seem like I wasn't even supposed to know about it. That led me to believe that I wasn't, so what's good?"

"Sound like you gotta take it up wit l'il bro then, and not come at me like I'm one of these other niggaz." He walked off after mugging Juice.

Juice smirked. "Yo, one day that nigga gone cause me to lose my respect for him, and when I do…" He made a gun with his forefinger and thumb. "Boom nigga." He blew on the fake gun and smiled.

I ain't like that analogy. Tywain was my mans and I wasn't about to let nothing happen to him if I could help it. "Yo, me giving you half of that kilo ain't gone fly right now. Me and the homey on something with that. What I can do is give you about nine ounces for you to get your grind on. After we make a few flips I'll hit you wit another nine."

Juice looked like I had just spit in his face. "A quarter kee. That's all you trying to come off of right now? Nigga fuck that!" He looked me up and down digusted.

Now my temper was starting to get the better of me. I tried my best to remain calm. I took a deep breath, and rolled my head around on my neck. "Bro, you know what? You my family, and I love you. Half of that kee is yours. Me and the homey a figure out how to make those loose ends meet. We gon' go pick it up and I'll meet you wherever you want to."

He smiled, and hugged me. "That's what I'm talking about, baby bro. It's about time we put our heads together, and don't even trip. I'm gone flip that half in about a week, then I'll get that back to you. How do that sound?"

I didn't even care. I was thinking about Blaze and the proposition she'd offered me. I weighed my options. I figured that if my brother didn't come through for me that I'd have her to fall back on anyway. I couldn't help but to look past his shoulder and I saw owe of them Blood niggaz trying to hug up on Shakia.

"Yo, that sound good, bro, we on." I walked past him and over to my woman. This fat nigga had her in a bear hug and she was telling him to let her go. Before I could make it to her she kneed him in the nuts. He hollered out like a l'il bitch and fell to his knees. One of his homeys, some skinny nigga with bumps all over his face, acted like he was about to smack her before I jumped in his path and stood face to face with him.

"Nigga, it ain't going down like that," I growled.

His niggaz surrounded me, and Tywain stepped into the circle. "On everything, you niggaz ain't on shit wit my mans right now. Y'all can back the fuck off of him, like right now!" He lifted his shirt and upped a Gauge.

"Whoa, Whoa, Whoa," Juice said, breaking into the circle. "That's my l'il brother right there, Slime." He backed them up and put his arm around my neck. "Bro, these my hitters from now on. You can't be beefing with them."

I wasn't hearing none of that. I wasn't about to let no muhfucka put they hands on Shakia in my presence. That was my l'il lady and I was standing on that shit. "Bro, don't nobody come over here and disrespect our women. I don't give a fuck who they is." I looked past him and mugged the shit out of them.

Juice nodded. "You right about that. But chill, I got them. Anyway, let's go get this merch so I can get right." He turned around to look at Shakia. "Damn, you got my l'il brother out here ready to get killed for you. You must be whipping his ass or something." He walked over to her and wrapped her in his arms.

She allowed that to take place for a brief second before she tried to get out of his embrace. "That ain't your business and let me go."

He trailed his hands down to her ass and cupped the cheeks. I had to catch myself as I watched him take advantage of her. She tried to fight him off, but he clung to her. I started to feel hot. My vision got blurry. He was laughing and kissing all over her face like it was cool.

I walked over to them and grabbed her out of his arms. "Shakia, take yo ass in the house and I'mma get up wit you later," I demanded.

She started to walk up to me, but changed her mind. She looked hurt and like she felt I was mad at her, but I wasn't. I was pissed at the fact that all the niggaz around me seemed like pussy ass rapists, all except my nigga Tywain. He looked digusted as hell. "Go in the house, I'll hit you up in a minute." She ran on to her porch, into the house, and slammed the door.

We passed a blunt back and forth while I drove and tried to get a hold of myself. Tywain sat in the passenger's seat with the Gauge on his lap. He looked irritated and pissed off.

"Yo, you got a right to feel how you feel. I shouldn't have told him that I was gone give him half because I promised that to you. Keeping shit one hunnit, you can still get the other half, bro, and I'll make shit happen another way."

Tywain shook his head. "Yo, fuck that dope, kid, it ain't about that. I'll eat crumbs out of the garbage can wit you, and you know that. What's fucking me up is your brother. Kid ain't right, and how he handled yo lady is fuck shit to me. I don't like them Blood niggaz either. All them fools just moved over from New Orleans. They sheisty as hell, and I see bullshit coming our way in the future. I fuck wit some real good Blood niggaz, that's my dogs. That branch out of New Orleans that moved into Black Haven just ain't it. Most of them niggaz is blow heads. They fuck niggaz, trust me."

I was trying to figure him out. "So, what you saying? You saying we shouldn't fuck wit Juice?" I was willing to roll wit my homey over my brother, because that nigga seemed like he was becoming more and more grimy. I didn't know what he could do wit a half a kilo wit all those mouths to feed that followed him now.

Tywain passed the blunt back to me and turned up his Lean. "Keeping shit real, I don't think we should because them niggas ain't gone do shit but snort that flake up. That's just my opinion, though. It ain't really worth getting into it with Juice over, so let's just give him this shit, and do our own thing. But mark my Words he gone be back once he see us on our feet shining.

That night Juice got his half of kilo, and me and Tywain branched off with the other half. His aunty cooked our half and turned it back into a full kee. Tywain had some of the l'il homeys from around his way sit up in the spot with us, and we bagged the whole kee up in dimes. It took us from two in the afternoon until 1 in the morning. When we got finished we hit the L'il homeys with a G sack apiece, and Tywain broke the game down to them. They were his l'il cousins so I let him holler at them while I formulated a plot in my own mind. My plan was to hustle every single day, spending no less than 12 hours a day in the spot for a full month. I had money on my mind, and that's just what me and the Homey did.

His aunt had tabs on all of the dope heads around town. We kept her smoking nice and she kept the back door to the apartment that we hustled out of, rocking. It seemed like fiends were there every other minute beating on the door and buying ten and twenty dimes at a time. It only took us two weeks to make over a hundred thousand dollars. You see we bagged up all dimes, that's $2800 per 28-gram ounce. Times that by the 36 ounces that we had and that's one hundred thousand and eight hundred dollars. We ain't take no shorts. That was the rule. We kept the product coming nice and lovely, and we ain't take no less that ten dollars. I didn't give a fuck if they came with ten dollars in pennies, I took it.

Tywain had this Russian kat that his grandfather had been in the services with. He was one of them older Russian dudes that really didn't mind black people, but he preferred his own race of people over any other kind. One day we were over Tywain's grandmother's crib, having a lovely Sunday dinner and he was over there visiting with Tywain's grandfather. Every Sunday we tried to get together and go over to the homey's grandparent's house, because his grandmother threw down in the kitchen. Her name was Lily, and his grandfather's name was Russell.

As soon as we pulled up to their house this day, we saw a brand-new black on black Hummer in the driveway. I thought it was kind of odd, but Tywain didn't pay it no mind.

"Bro, who Hummer is that? I know yo people ain't rolling like that."

He opened the door to my whip and shook his head. "Grandpops friend Serge. He a Russian dude that was with my old man in the services back in the day." We walked me toward the house. "Come on, he cool as hell. And plus, I wanna drop this hundred thousand in his lap. I know he'll treat us real nice for it."

Before I could even make it into the house, I could smell Lily's famous cornbread. That cornbread was so good and so sweet that often times I would eat two and three pieces of it before I would touch anything else.

"Bro, make sure you remember that we still gotta fuck wit Bell on the Loud tip. Shorty been hitting my phone all afternoon telling me to come by."

Tywain nodded as we walked into the house and Lily bum rushed us with hugs and kisses. She was about five feet even, and had a nice shape on her for an older woman. Her wig was all gray, and she was the most loving woman I had ever met before. She spoke her mind and loved the Lord. She hugged me and kissed my cheeks.

"Boy, lean that head down here so I can get me some sugar." I heard her lips smack against my jaw. "That's what I'm talking about. I'm so happy to see y'all. That's one thing that I depend on after church every Sunday is to see you and my grandbaby. These streets are getting crazier. The devil is alive and roaming. He's searching for souls to devour, and I thank Jesus that he ain't did nothing to one of y'all. Praise the Lord for that."

"Woman, would you stop with all that holy rolling." Russell said, coming into the room with a belly so big it looked like he was already full.

He was a skinny man, but it was odd because his gut stuck all the way out. He was dark skinned with serious eyes. He had a smooth face that had little specks of gray hair that he must of missed while he was shaving.

He was extremely military. He spoke with a loud booming voice, and whenever he sat down, it looked like he had a stick up his butt. "We been in church all day long. The last thing I wanna do is come home and continue the discussion. Jesus know that we love him, and we agree that he died for our sins. It's time to eat and if you're in here messing with them then that mean that the food ain't being prepared right. That ain't fair."

She rolled her eyes at him and shook her head. "I don't know how I been with you for 40 years. 40 long years, too. You done stole all of my youth away." She chuckled, straightening her wig and running her hands over her hips. Her dress was so colorful that I damn near needed sunglasses.

"Stole yo youth?" His eyes bugged out of his bead. "Girl,

when I met you I was captain of the football team. I had all of the fine mamma jammas trying to get a piece of the pie until you threw it in the street and ran it over with that old Lincoln your father had given you in junior high." He shook his head as if he were thinking back on those days. "I was flier than Superfly back then. Shaft ain't have nothing on me. "

She laughed so hard that she passed gas. "Excuse me, gentlemen, but I don't know what that war did to Russell's brain. You might have been captain of the football team, but the team was so bad that us girls beat y'all two years in a row. Lucky, it was just for fun and not recorded for stats, because if it was that would have been embarrassing even to this day. And Superfly is a stretch. Wasn't none of the girls at our school thinking about you. The only reason my father let me go out with you is because you had so many bumps on your face he knew I'd never let you touch me."

"Well he'd a lost that bet. You were so fast that all I had to do was buy you a hotdog and five minutes later we were butt naked in the back seat of your father's car. Boy, to be butt naked in the back seat of your father's car. Boy to be young, wild and free again." He smacked her so hard on her booty that she yelped. "Shut up, that was all diaper. Now get your tail in there and make that dinner!"

She walked away with a face so red that I could tell she was embarrassed. Tywain lowered his head and put a hand over his eyes as if to say he didn't know what was going on.

"Well, well, well, y'all come over to eat us out of a house and home or what?" Russell asked after shaking our hands. He had a grip that hurt so bad I wanted to punch him in his dentures.

Tywain hugged him. "Yeah, Pops, you know we gotta stop by every Sunday to get a decent meal. I also want to discuss a little business with Serge, if that's okay with you."

I was listening to what they were saying, but for the most part I watched Lily navigate through the kitchen like a pro. She had her head in the oven for one second, then she was frosting a cake, and from there she was peeling corn. I was amazed and I appreciated her.

Russell led us downstairs, and into his den where there was a skinny white, bald headed dude sitting on the couch smoking a cigar, and talking on his phone. When we walked into the room he hung up, and stood up. He had to be about 6 feet 6 inches tall. "Tywain, how have you been, son? "He grabbed him and hugged him tightly.

Tywain hugged him back, and patted his back, before they released each other. "It's good to see you. I want to talk a little business with you." They sat down on the side of each other before Tywain hopped back up and introduced me and him. "This is my best friend, Taurus, and my right-hand man."

Serge shook my hand and eyed me closely. "You have to be careful of those you call your friend. A friend is willing to die for you at the drop of a hat. A friend will be there for you when no one else is. And to say that one is your right hand, that means that you cannot function properly without this person the same way most people cannot function without the use of both hands." He sat down next to Tywain. "Are you telling me that all of these things are true for this one that you call your right hand?"

Tywain looked over at me and frowned. "You damn right it is."

He nodded. "Then all should be well. Tell me what can I do for you?" He puffed on his cigar, and handed another one to Russell. "These are fresh from Crimeria. The best in all of the land of Russia."

Russell ran the cigar under his nose and sniffed it. "Smells good. Toss me that lighter."

As the room clouded up with smoke, Tywain lit a cigarette.

"I have 80 thousand dollars, and I want to put it into your lap. I want half Coke, and I want half of that Russian Meth that we spoke about last year."

Serge puffed on his cigar and looked at the ceiling. He crossed his legs and gave Russell a weird look that I could not decipher. Russell nodded and turned his head away. "Why do you think that you are ready to lie down in the bed with me? To what do I owe this invitation?"

Tywain was silent for a brief moment. "I'm ready to make something happen for myself, and my brother right here is as well." We both nodded in agreeance.

Serge sat forward on the couch, and stubbed out his cigar in the ashtray. "$80,000 is peanuts to me. It's not really worth the time to get involved with gang bangers. I have bigger fish to fry than something so senseless." He waved him off. "I'm not interested."

Russell blew the smoke from his cigar to the ceiling. "What are you trying to do grandson?"

Tywain still had his eyes on Serge. He looked a little offended, and like he wanted to say something to the man. Serge was already watching a hockey game on the big screen television. He didn't look like he had a care in the world. I think that irritated Tywain even more. "I want to invest this $80,000 into something that's going to bring us back a nice return. It's time that I do something with my life. I want to open a few barbershops, and maybe even a restaurant or something, but I can't do that if I don't have the capital."

Russell rubbed his chin, and looked over at Tywain closely. "Do you have the money with you?"

Tywain nodded.

"I'll tell you what. You give me some time to discuss things over with Serge, and I'll give you my decision of what we'll do after dinner. For now, I'd like for you boys to leave the room, so we can talk business."

An hour later, we were all sitting around the dinner table with Serge smacking so loud that I couldn't do nothing but stare at him. Russell was just as bad. Serge had a spoon in one hand and a fork in the other. He'd fork up his macaroni and cheese and stuff his mouth with a spoonful of rice at the same time.

"You know what I like about the blacks the most?"

"What's that?" Russell asked biting into his pork chop and ripping the meat from the bone. His hands were so greasy that he had a hard time holding his glass of red wine in his hands. He chewed his food with his mouth wide open. It sounded like he was chewing a mouth full of gum.

"You women put their passion and soul into the meals and it makes it taste so much better. There is a reason that I am here every Sunday without fail. It is because it is the one time out of the week that I am able to feed the heart in my stomach. I'd marry Lily if I could." He smiled at her, then stuffed his mouth with food.

I didn't know that the Russian came over to their house every Sunday because this had been the first time I'd ever seen him. He must have came over way before me and Tywain usually got there. You see, we usually got there just in time to pick up the plates that Lily had for us. So, Serge must of got there early enough to eat with them every Sunday, and then left right away. I didn't know at that time, but I made a mental note to peep his antics.

"Well, thank you, Serge. It sho' is nice to feel appreciated. I wish some of that good nature would rub off on my husband. Lord knows I ain't got a thank you from him in nearly a year." She looked sad, and kept her eyes on her plate.

Russell burped. "Woman, I'll never thank you for what you're supposed to be doing. That's your job, just like me bringing home the bacon. Do you tell me thank you every time?"

"Yes, I do," she said, matter-of-factly.

Russell was quiet for a moment. "Well, I guess you got me there." He burped, and covered his mouth way too late.

I tripped off of them for the next half hour. They went back and forth, throwing shots at each other until I got bored and removed myself from the table. When it was all said and done, Russell plugged us with four kilos of cocaine, and four of meth. It was for me and Tywain to hit the ground running and that's exactly what we did.

Ghost

Chapter 10

Shakia was sitting in my car when I came out one morning to get my phone that I had left inside of it the night before. Me and Tywain had been hustling day in and day out for two months straight and the only time I saw Shakia was when I was coming or going. I knew that I was neglecting her to a certain extent, but I was grinding, and I didn't have nothing on my mind other than money. I was trying to master the whole meth part of the game, because more and more people were venturing out and getting acquainted with that drug in Memphis. I think that me and Tywain were the first to bring it to the hood. We started out by giving away a free dime bag of it with every fifty dollars of crack that someone bought. I think we must have tricked off an entire half of kee of meth, and before we knew it, the fiends were coming to purchase that instead of the crack. It was a cold way to flip the game upside down.

One of the Asian homies that I went to school with was a fool with whipping it. He would take the dope that we got from Russell and make it ten times more potent with a few ingredients that he got from the drug store. Before we knew it, me and Tywain had him and three of his female cousins on the payroll. We rented them out a trailer Where they could take our already potent meth and strengthen it three times over.

His name was Wango. He was about 5 feet 3 inches tall. Real skinny, and all the teeth in his mouth were false. He had a real habit for the drug, but as long as he had been working for me and Tywain there had never been a problem.

Wango had two female cousins that were also meth heads. They were very skinny, and their faces looked sunken in. I could not tell if one point in time they had been fine or whatever, because they were so hideous looking in the present, and both of their asses were as flat as a chopping board. That didn't matter to Wango though. Majority of the time I came over to the trailer, they were all walking around ass naked. I didn't know if him and them got down, but I assumed so.

Wango had the ins on all of the meth heads in town. It was like they had their own community. There were two sections of Memphis where the drug was wildly popular, and the Asians ran one section. The other section was ran by the gay community.

Both communities would literally kill you if you didn't have the pass to be over there at any given time. Wango was our in for the Asian side of town. It seemed that every one of them knew him, or knew of him. We'd fill his backpack up with the product, and he'd be gone for three whole days. When he returned he'd have over two hundred thousand dollars minimum. The Asians were getting us rich, and it was a section of town that we had to concentrate on because they also had a gang that ran through that community that called themselves the Asian Bloodz, and they didn't like nothing that was black. Wango told us that they had hemmed him up on numerous occasions asking about me and Tywain. He said that it was in our best interest to sit down with them, so that's what me and Tywain had done.

The meeting had ended at three in the morning. I was so tired when I got back that I had left my phone in the car. I was thinking about the sweet deal that we had landed with them when I ran into Shakia sitting in my whip going through my phone.

I nearly broke my neck getting to the door and whipping it open. "What the hell is you doing, shorty? That ain't for us," I said grabbing my phone out of her hand, and looking at her like I was so disappointed, which I was.

She tried to grab it back out of my hand. "Stop, I wasn't even thinking about what you had going on in there. I was on Facebook seeing what was popping." She rolled her eyes and crossed her arms over her chest. "Why have you been avoiding me again,

Taurus?"

I didn't feel like getting into no long ass argument with her. I was still very tired from the night before and I had to get a little sleep so I could finish grinding with the homey. She looked like she was wide awake and ready to fight all night.

"Look Shakia, I don't feel like arguing with you about shit that don't matter. I'm tired right now, and I'm gon' have to holler at you later. Come on, let's go, "I said trying to get her out of my car by grabbing her hand.

She jerked it away. "When did you start cursing at me? And why is the only time I see you is when we're screwing? What type of bull is that? "I could see the tears falling down her cheeks and I tried to compose myself. I hated to see a female cry.

"Look, I'm just tired right now. I ain't mean to cuss at you. You know I care about you more than that."

"Care? What happened to you loving me?" she asked, getting out of the car and walking up on me.

I took a step back and exhaled loudly. "Shakia, look, ma, you know I love you. You my girl, and I'll do anything for you. It's just that I'm tired and I got a lot on my plate right now. I ain't trying to front on you, and I still got your back against all odds. It's just right now that I need to go in the house and get some rest. I'll holler at you first thing in the afternoon." I hugged her briefly, and walked toward the crib. I could already imagine my head hitting the pillow.

"I'm pregnant."

I kept walking, because I ain't think I heard her correctly. I knew my mind had to be playing tricks on me. I got on to my porch and started to open the door. The crickets were still chirping, which was weird because it had to be about eight in the morning.

"Did you hear me, Taurus? I said I'm pregnant, and you're the father." I could hear in her voice that she was on the verge of breaking down.

I did a complete 180. "What did you just say?" I had heard her, but a part of me needed to hear it again. The reality of what she'd said didn't register to my brain. She walked up to me, and lifted her shirt.

"I'm pregnant. We're going to have a baby. I need to know what you want me to do." She looked at me, her face wet with tears.

I swallowed just from seeing how it was emotionally hurting her. One thing was for certain, there was no bitch in me. A bitch to me was a chump that got a woman pregnant and then crapped all over her and the kid. I wasn't that type. I believed in standing firm as a man on my responsibility. I didn't care if she had been a chick that I had only screwed once, and had never met prior to that, she would have been straight just because I knew there was a possibility that I was the father of her child.

"What do you mean? I'm about to hold you down and make sure that you're straight. I know that when I hit the pussy you were a virgin. I ain't use no rubber, and I never have to this day. I got you." I wrapped her in my arms and kissed her forehead.

She couldn't just let things stay there. That wasn't the type of person Shakia was. She just had to push the envelope. "Taurus, I don't want our child to be born in a destructive household. I want our child to have both of us. I want you to settle down with me, and leave those streets alone. I'm tired of worrying about you every single day and not seeing you for days at a time." She took a step back and looked me in the eyes. "Now you know that my dream was to attend Texas State, and to become an attorney. I always said that there would be nothing that would stand in the way of that. But then, you came. Now I'm still going to get my education, it's just that a baby makes it more difficult. We'll need to handle our business fifty-fifty. That will be the only way that we can make it out of this day to day struggle. I need for you to be all mine, and our child's, or I'll figure this out on my own."

I didn't know what to say to that. She was laying so much on me at one time that my brain felt like it wanted to shut down. One thing was for sure; I was going to take care of my kid by all means. I didn't know if I was ready to settle down and just be with her though, and the more she pressured me, the more I was sure I was not ready for all of that and I told her exactly what I was thinking.

"Shakia, I love you, and no matter what I'm going to be there for you and my child. As long as I have breath in my body, you will never have to worry about anything if I can help it. But just like I told you before, I'm not ready to settle down with nobody. I'm still trying to get my weight up, and get these streets out of my system. You givin' me an ultimatum ain't gon' do nothing but push me away from you."

She looked like she was ready to snap. "What the fuck is in them streets that I can't give you? Why do you keep on running to them like you're missing something? Don't you know that that living only has two roads? You'll either wind up in prison or dead in the grave yard. Due to the fact that I'm having your child, I would rather for you to work a nine to five and come home to us every night." She frowned. "You got all of that common sense, but you still act dumb. Don't you get it?"

I was getting so irritated, that I was about to walk off on her ass. A lot of the stuff she was saying made sense, but when I got down to the nitty gritty of it all, it really didn't because who was going to pay my mom's bills? Who was going to make sure that my brothers and sister was taken care of on all ends of the spectrum? Who was going to take care of me and make sure that I was straight? And now that I had a child on the way who was going to provide for it and its mother? Nobody but me!

"The system is designed for you to fail, and you're falling

right into their trap, and you're too stupid to see that." She crinkled her face. "God, I can't believe you. I thought you were so different, but you're nothing but a D-boy like the rest of these short-term winners, and long-term losers around here. You know what, I'll figure things out on my own. I can't even look at you." She turned around and jogged to her house.

I went into mine and crashed onto the bed, and was out like a light. I didn't know how to feel about the situation. I kind of chopped it up to being another load to carry on my shoulders. One way or the other, I would make it happen. I was certain of that.

That same day me and Tywain had a sit down with one of the well-known transsexuals that ran the gay community on the east side of Memphis. He insisted that we meet him at his club, even though I tried to get out of that. The last thing I wanted to see was a bunch of men dressed up like women doing the most.

I didn't have nothing against that population, I just didn't wanna see that shit. I guess they would feel the same way about walking into a strip club that featured nothing but women, but then again, I didn't know. My knowledge of their people was very limited. All I knew is that he was standing in the way of us making a lot of money, so it was crucial to get him on deck. With me having a baby on the way that made me know that I had to go ten times harder. I wasn't turning my collar down to nothing or no one.

The dude's name was Starburst. He was about 5 feet 9 inches tall, and had fake breasts, and I could only guess ass injections as well, because his overall frame was very skinny, and those additions to his body looked disproportioned. He had a golden wig on his head and so much make up on that he looked like an opera singer. He escorted us to a booth in his strip club. It had not opened for business that night yet, and I was hoping that we could conclude things before it did. I couldn't imagine what went on in them types of places, but I didn't want to find out. As he walked in front of me he tried to switch his hips so hard that he damn wear fell over. I scanned the club and saw that it looked like a normal strip club, but just more colorful.

As we slid into the booth, one of his fellow transsexual waitresses, brought us over a bottle of champagne. Tywain grabbed it out of the ice and popped the bottle. He didn't seem like he cared about being in there. He grabbed one of the glasses off of the table and filled it. Starburst held up a glass to him and he filled his glass up too. This made the man smile. Tywain offered me the bottle and I declined. I just couldn't get comfortable in that atmosphere. I think it was because while growing up, my father had always told me that gay people were going to burn in hell. He often recited the part of the bible where Sodom and Gomorrah was destroyed by God. He said that those that mingled with gay people were also sure to burn in hell. I didn't understand that he was trying to scare me and my siblings until I got older, but sometimes old habits were hard to break.

Starburst took a sip from his champagne and left lipstick on the rim. "So, tell me, fellas, what do you want to talk about?" He looked from Tywain to me, after flipping his long gold hair over his shoulders.

"We wanna talk about a compromise. Word is that the LGBT community bows down to your feet, and that you run it. We understand that nothing can come in or out of this side of town without going through you. The reason that we are here is because we want to make you a proposition," I said, looking him straight in the eye.

He took another sip of his champagne, and fluttered his eyelashes that were so long they looked ridiculous. "I'm all ears."

Tywain cut in, "Well, seeing as the new drug choice around here is meth, what do you say we kick you in ten percent of all of our profits from your community. That's ten percent of any bag sold on your turf. We're also willing to bump that up to fifteen percent if you would be willing to promote our product."

Starburst refilled his glass and gave us a look that said he wasn't impressed. "Chile, those numbers don't sound so right to me. Now I know a whole lot of people that are doing Ice, and I know the money is good. I have constructed a whole community, and my bitches don't fuck with nothing unless I give my stamp of approval. If you want that stamp of approval you gone have to give me 25 percent of all the proceeds from my people. That's including promoting and everything. Now if that don't sound right to you then I will find other businessmen to deal with." He smacked his lips and cleaned the lipstick off of his teeth while looking in a mirror he pulled out
of his purse.

I wasn't willing to give this stud no fucking 25 percent. I felt like he was trying to gangsta us while wearing a dress. That was making me feel some type of way.

Tywain rubbed his chin, and looked like he was mulling things over. "Let me ask you something, how many people would you say that you bring to the table that would become our customers? Give me a ballpark estimation?"

Starburst shrugged his shoulders. "Four hundred, give or take a few. And these aren't your average dope fiends. Everybody in this community got good jobs. Our money flow would be consistent.

My mind was blown after I heard how many potential customers we would have. I got to seeing all kinds of numbers in my head that had me smiling from ear to ear. I felt like Tywain was on to something, and I was grateful that Russell had got us the sit down with Starburst. It looked like it was going to turn out to be extremely beneficial.

"You boys must know that I don't usually step outside of my people for nothing. But your product comes highly recommended and plus we respect Russell. Therefore, I'm willing to give you the key to my portion of the city, but it's gone cost you a little bit. I'm sure that in the end you will be very happy." He sat back and rubbed his hands together.

Tywain leaned over into my ear. "Yo, kid, I'm telling you that it don't get no better than this. We closed the deal with the Asian Bloodz, now we close this one and we'll be seeing them numbers. I say let's do it. That's still 75 percent of 400 customers. We can't lose."

I agreed and we closed the deal right then and there. We gave Starburst an ounce of our product, and he gave us V.I.P. passes to Bad and Bougie, which was a straight strip club on the other side of town. "My sister runs that joint. Her name is Trixie. She about her paper and looking for a weed plug. If you can find somebody that's heavy in that department that'll be another plus for you. Make sure you tell her that I sent you. I'll hit her up on Facebook later. The only thing I ask is that you respect my people, and that you treat us fairly. You do that, and you'll have loyalty standing behind you one hundred percent, trust me. Do we understand each other?" He asked standing up.

We nodded in unison. It ended with us giving him a brief hug before walking out of the door just as the parking lot was filling up. It was ironic because that same night we ran into Well.

I was at the stop light on Townsend, ready to turn on to the freeway when she pulled up alongside of my whip beating so hard that I felt like she flexed on me. She was in a money green Benz truck that sat high on gold rims. She had all blue ground effects under her truck, and all through the interior all you could see was televisions. I was instantly jealous. She waved me down and told me to pull over.

We wound up at the Chicken Shack, which was a ghetto chicken joint that specialized in down home chicken. I felt like it was the best in Memphis. I liked how crispy their chicken was, and all of the sides were always on point. The only thing about the place was that it was smacked dead in the hood, and the area was known for jackers. To say I wasn't worried would have been a lie, and I had a .40 caliber on me, and I knew that Tywain was double breasted. That didn't matter to me. I felt like we were making some powerful moves and the last thing we needed was to get into some bullshit.

We sat all the way in the back of the place. Well had two big niggas that were in her truck with her. They were dark skinned and looked like they weighed 300 pounds apiece, if not more. They were her bodyguards, and you could tell they were strapped by the handles that poked out of their black wife beaters.

She ordered a platter of chicken, and a big thing of macaroni and cheese for the whole table. I started feeling her swag again. For a big girl, I was so attracted to her that I couldn't take my eyes off of her. Now don't get it twisted, I ain't have nothing against bigger women, I just hadn't had one before, but I was feeling her like a muhfucka.

She smiled and her dimples appeared on her cheeks. "So, what's good, Playboy? I thought you was gone fuck wit me some more?" She grabbed a piece of chicken, and tore the skin off, before putting it in her mouth and crunching.

I squirted Purell on my hands and rubbed them together. I was about to dive into that food with no remorse. "I been handling business on other ends, but I'm ready to fuck wit you right now." I grabbed a drumstick and drenched it with hot sauce before tearing it up. It tasted so good that before I finished with that piece I grabbed another one.

"Alright then, let's talk numbers. What you working with?" she asked spooning macaroni into her mouth. "I can handle anything." Her goon stayed on the lookout for danger. I could tell that they were ready for something to pop off, like they were familiar with the area or something.

Tywain sucked his fingers. "You got that good Loud, am I right?"

She burped and wiped her mouth with a napkin. "My shit so loud that you need ear plugs to fuck wit it." She bit off of a drumstick then grabbed her pop off of the table, sipping it through the straw.

We heard a series of gunshots somewhere outside and the whole table got to grabbing for their guns except her. She looked like she didn't have a care in the world. She continued to chew while we rubber necked to see if we could see what was going on outside.

After it seemed like the moment had passed, Tywain put his pistol back on his waist. "What them pounds going for?" He opened the top of his pop container and drank it like that.

"I'll tell you what, since I fuck with Taurus over here, I'll do y'all real nice. Just give me a number and let me see what you trying to do."

"Twenty bands," I said, wiping my mouth wit a napkin. "What you a do for that?" Outside we heard more gunfire, and then the squealing of tires. By this time all of us had our guns out and were headed toward the front of the restaurant. I was ready to body anything that looked like it could have been a threat. Well didn't move.

"Look, mane, y'all know we in Orange Mound and them niggaz always bussing at something. That shit ain't got nothing to do with us. Now, let's talk business so I can see where thangs go."

After we made sure everything was good, we sat back at the table and closed a deal. She did us real nice for that twenty, and by the end of that day me and Tywain had made a few power moves.

Ghost

Chapter 11

Juice started tooting powder real hard after he got involved with the Bloodz from New Orleans. It got so bad that damn near every time I saw him he had it in his system. Because he was always high, I felt it clouded his judgment and caused him to act differently.

I was hustling so hard that me and him barely hung together. He never said nothing about the half of kilo I'd loaned him, so I didn't either. I wasn't tripping on it, and whatever I felt he had going on was not my concern. I was familiar with my brother being a stomp down hustler on all levels. But after his use of the powder he became lazier, and the only thing on his mind was robbing somebody. I wasn't on that because I was out there pounding the pavement with Tywain. Now don't get me wrong, if I felt like there would have been an opportunity where I could have hit a lick that would have put me way ahead, with low risk of retaliation then I would have been all for it. I just wasn't in a position to be in drama with nobody because I couldn't beef and make money, every real hustler knew that.

One day, I came into the house and this fool was sitting at the table tooting cocaine off of a plate. At first, I couldn't believe my eyes, because I just knew I was seeing things. I walked past him and didn't say anything.

I went to my little sister's room and pushed in the door. I saw her laying on her stomach doing homework, so I stepped inside and closed the door. "Hey l'il mama. How are you doing?"

As soon as she saw that it was me, she jumped up and ran to me. I picked her up and she wrapped her arms around my neck.

"I missed you so much, big brother." She kissed me on the cheek. "I thought you said you was gon' take me shopping?" She poked out her lip and crossed her arms over her chest.

I pulled her to me and hugged her. "I still am. Have I ever lied to you about anything?"

"No, but this could be the first time, and I was worried that you forgot. All of the girls at my school are wearing Elie Saab, and I'm not. It's already hard enough to be a freshman, and this isn't making it any easier you know."

I had been grinding so hard that I didn't even realize at that time that my little sister was already in the ninth grade. I felt like the worst big brother ever. "Hey…what if I just gave you the money for it, would that be cool?"

She shook her head. "Hell no! You said that you were going to take me shopping. I want to spend some time with you because you never spend any time with me. Don't you love me like you do momma?" she asked looking sad.

I grabbed her and kissed her on the forehead. "You already know that you're my baby girl, so don't even ask me no bull crap like that again."

"I'm just saying, because you never take me anywhere. After a while that starts to mess with a girl's self-esteem. You make me feel like I'm hideous or something." She sat on the edge of her bed and grabbed her laptop.

"I'll tell you what, after I go out here and holler at Juice, me and you are going to spend the day together. How about that?"

Her eyes lit up. She jumped off of the bed and into my arms wrapping her legs around me, like she used to when she was a little girl. "That sounds awesome! I can't wait." She hugged my neck tightly, planting butterfly kisses on me, I sat her down.

Kneeling between her legs, and looking into her eyes as I held her hands. "Mary, tell me something. How many times have you seen Juice sitting at the table, snorting dope like that?"

She shrugged her shoulders. "Way more than I can count. He does it all the time. Most of the time when I come home from school that's what he's doing. At first it scared me, but now it doesn't bother me at all." She turned her head to the side. "Why do you ask?"

I shook my head, irritated. "Because that's not something that you're supposed to be seeing as a little girl. You deserve to have a fair chance in life, and it's our job to make sure that you have as many opportunities lined up as possible."

"But I'm not a little girl anymore. I'm all grown up. All the boys look at me different, and Gotto says that I'm very mature."

I wanted to snap about the boy's comment she made, but I decided to let her have that argument for the day. My sister was well developed for the age of 13. She looked like a little woman, and that fact scared me, because there were so many predators in the world. You could literally not tell that she was the age she was until she opened her mouth. Only then could you detect her immaturity. I would go ballistic if I ever found out any boy, or man for that matter, had put their hands on my sister in any way. I was not playing about her. She was the spitting image of my mother, and that alone made me looney over her.

"What I'm saying is that you should be able to come home and not see things like that, because it's not normal. So, what I'm going to do is go out here and holler at him and you can get ready and wait for me in my car. You got that?"

She jumped off of the bed looking very happy, and then all at once her mood seemed to change. I could detect a sense of worry in her face.

"What's the matter, baby girl?" I asked wrapping her into my arms. From the time she was a little baby, she'd always been so special to me.

"I just don't want you to go out there and get into a fight with him. He's gotten very mean since dad got locked up. I am afraid of him now." She confessed nervously, as she bit on her finger-nails.

"You ain't got nothing to worry about. Just grab your phone, and I'll be outside in a minute."

As soon as she left out of the front door I closed and locked it. I walked back into the living room where my brother was just picking his head up from the plate. He took a glass of alcohol and drank it slow. I guessed washing down the remnants of the cocaine. When he took a long swallow from the glass he sat back in his chair, and ran his hand over his face.

"Taurus, what up, l'il nigga?"

I felt disgusted by the sights of him. His dreds looked like they had not been retwisted in nearly a year. His clothes looked worn out and dirty. I saw that his fingernails had dirt caked up under them. He just looked like a total mess.

"Bro, what the fuck you doin'?" I asked, feeling my temper rise.

He shrugged his shoulders. "What you talkin' about?"

"I'm talking about you sitting here in our mother's house snorting dope like that shit cool or something. You don't care about our little sister seeing you like that?"

"Seeing me like what?" He ran his hand over his nappy dreds. "Everybody snort dope. It's like smoking a cigarette," he said, pulling one out and lighting it. "And this ain't momma house. This muhfucka still belong to my father. She don't pay no bills up in here like that. Just because he locked up right now don't mean that this spot ain't his."

I sidestepped that argument. "Bro, if you can, can you please not do this shit at the living room table? I don't like our little sister seeing this kind of stuff. She's too young for that. In fact, if I can help it I don't want her being around nothing like this period. We're the only ones that are going to protect her, so if we don't then who will?"

He scratched his scalp for a full minute it seemed like without responding. Afterward I saw a big clump of dandruff in his nail that he popped toward the ceiling. I don't know where it went, but had it hit me I would have snapped. "To be honest with you I don't give a fuck what she see. That ain't my daughter, that's just my sister. And nine times out of ten, her nigga gon' toot powder. I don't know why you stress yourself out over shit that don't matter. She's a girl, somebody gon' eventually corrupt her." He was talking like he words were gospel and made all the sense in the world. It was hard for me to realize sometimes that we were really siblings. What the hell?

Had he not been my brother I would have popped him right then and there. The way he spoke about our sister like she was just another female on the street made me want to body his ass. In my eyes, my sister was pure and special. I was not going to let her get sucked into the ghetto. I was going to make it my business to ensure that she went to college and became whatever she wanted to become. Her future was more important to me than my own.

"You know what, Juice, I don't even know what to say to you right now because that dope got you all fucked up. You're talking about a thirteen-year-old girl as if she's trash, and you don't care, yet you stand up for our father who can defend his own honor. I ain't feeling you right now, so I'm gone leave this house before we tear this muhfucka up." I felt my chest heaving up and down and my vision getting hazy. I made my way to the front door and found my little sister there with tears in her eyes.

"All I give a fuck about is me, Taurus. If you live by that then you ain't gotta worry about getting hurt. I ain't responsible for nobody other than me."

I slammed the door behind us and wrapped my arm around my sister. "It's okay, baby girl. No matter what I got you, and I'll always have you until the day I die. You understand that?" I asked kneeling down in front of her and looking into her eyes. She looked so innocent. I felt a strong protection for my sister in my heart.

"Yes, I understand, and I love you so much, Taurus." We hugged before heading to my whip.

Just as I opened the door for her my mother pulled up in her small Neon. She blew the horn and I walked over to see what she wanted.

"I need to talk to you, Taurus. Where are you about to go?" she asked stepping out of her car and hugging me.

"I'm finna take Mary shopping like I promised her a long time ago. Why, what's the matter?" I could sense that there was something bothering her.

She took a step back and lowered her head. "The rent, the landlord been over here three times now and I been ducking him. I was wondering if you were going to help me out until I could figure something else out?" She looked embarrassed.

"Damn, I forgot about that. That's my fault, momma." I went into my pocket and gave her about five thousand dollars in cash. "That's for your pocket, and this is for the rent and stuff." I gave her another five gees. "Don't you ever feel embarrassed to come and get what you need from me. You're my baby, right?"

She nodded her head and a tear fell down her cheeks. "Yes, I am, and I love you so much." She hugged me tight.

"From now on you give dude my phone number and tell him to get in contact with me when the rent gotta be paid. That goes for all of the bills. Period. You ain't gotta worry about none of that no more. I got this." I kissed her forehead. "Go get in the car and I'mma take you shopping too."

I ran into the house and closed the door to our bedroom. I needed to hit my stash before I hit up the mall. There was a slit on the side of my mattress where I stuffed bands of money. I didn't have all of my chips there because me and Tywain was constantly reinvesting our paper back into the business. I had about fifty gees in ten thousand-dollar bundles. I reached into it and pulled out one of them. I was down to thirty now because I had just given my mother ten thousand. But I had another $80,000 in the safe at Tywain's mother's house, so I was good. Plus, we had a nice amount of product, that was ice, cocaine, and Loud. A total street value of about 500 thousand.

I knew I wasn't in a position to be spending money, because I had this quota in my mind that I was trying to hit before I spent anything. I wanted to have 500 thousand in cash, and 500 thousand in dope, that was after Tywain took his cut on all three ends.

One thing about the game, in order to survive in it you had to keep reinvesting. The more product you had, the more money you would be able to make. Those that started spending right away wound up going in circles. They never moved ahead. The most embarrassing thing for a real hustler to do was to go and cop the same amount of product every time they went to buy some. The game was designed for you to advance each time, not for you to constantly remain in the same place. I was one of those trappers that believed in saving money. I wanted to make it out of the dope game and into the corporate world in some sort of way. I wanted to own my own property and businesses and make sure that my family was well taken care of, especially the women because they had nobody to protect them. But I saw the game as a crutch, not as a lifetime job. I was going to use it to launch me into a better position, so I knew I had to move very strategically.

I let my mother and sister go crazy in that mall. We had originally came in for one Elie Saab dress that my sister just had to have, but in less than one hour. They had so many bags in their hands that it looked like we'd gone grocery shopping. My mother was worse than my sister. She was running in and out of stores, and then pulling me into them where I would come out of my pocket and purchase whatever she wanted. It felt good to see the smile on her face. It made me feel like a man. I don't think I had ever seen her so happy.

My sister was just as bad, but she was a little more sensible.

I bought her a ten Elie Saab dresses. She also got a lot of Fendi and Prada. We wound up using that whole ten I gave my mother earlier, plus the ten I'd bought with me, and later once we got back to the house I gave it back to her. All I cared about was making them happy, and I feel like I accomplished that.

We strolled into the house at about nine that night. My brother, Gotto, opened the door, and when he saw all of those bags his eyes got so big that I thought they were going to roll out of his head. The women squeezed past him and went into their rooms slamming their doors after thanking me and kissing me on both cheeks.

I was about to head out when he grabbed my arm. At first it caught me off guard because I didn't like nobody touching me. I didn't care if they were family or not. I yanked my arm away and looked at him like he was crazy.

"Damn, bro, calm down. I just need to holler at you real quick," he said taking his wife beater off and throwing it on the couch in the front room. He was heavyset as hell and I could never understand why he was so quick to take his shirt off. Bro had muscles in his arms, but his stomach took the glory away from all of that, and he swore up and down that he was swole.

I was ready to hit the bricks. I didn't feel like getting into a discussion with him. Me and my little brother didn't really jam like that. He was a little weird to me. All he seemed to care about was white girls and being a part of that circle. He very rarely spoke about his own race.

"What's good, l'il bro? I'm on my way to handling some business, so what's up?" I made
sure I let him know all of that because he was a talker and I ain't feel like chatting wit nobody right then.

"That's exactly what I wanna talk to you about." He sat down on the couch. "Business."

My phone vibrated in my hand. It was a text from Blaze asking if I was available to talk. I texted that I would be in five minutes and that I would call her. Looking down at my brother, I took a seat across from him.

"What about it?"

"Bro, I need to do something for myself. I need for you to put me on." He leaned forward on the couch, almost invading my personal space.

"Bro, hustling ain't for everybody. I thought you was doing the school thing?"

"I am, but I need some cash flow, big bro. Everybody around here eating except me. I'm ready to make things happen for myself too." He pulled out a Black and Mild, and put fire to the tip of the cigar.

I grabbed it out of his mouth. "Man, my momma back there. How you finna smoke in the house while she in her room? What type of respect is that?" I was irritated. I didn't know how him or Juice viewed my mother, but I didn't like how they behaved while she was present or somewhere in the house.

"Damn, Taurus, chill. She don't even care about all of that. I already asked her and she said it was cool." He wiped the sweat off of his forehead. "Bro, put me on. I need to get some cash."

I knew off the rip that I wasn't fucking with him on no narcotics tip. I didn't wanna throw him a bone at all, but he had the kind of personality that he would keep on bugging you in subtle ways until it drove you crazy.

"Bro, what you trying to do?" I asked rubbing my temples. I felt like it was a bad idea, but I wanted to get it over with.

He looked as if he couldn't control his self. "You know I'm always messing around at them college parties, right. Well, what if you plugged me with some coke, and I could pop it off for you. Or you could give me some so I could just get on myself?"

I shook my head so quick that he wasn't even done talking

and I didn't care. "That shit ain't happening. But what I will do is let you pop some of this Loud. I'mma set you up with a gee pack. You just bring me back 200 and you keep the 8. I'm gone give you a list of clients that you can make deliveries to. You pop 16 ounces in a week, and I'll give you your own four ounces for you to do whatever you please with. Every time you make a G for me I'll give you an ounce for yourself until you're on your feet and I'll double whatever you spend. Now if I see that you can't handle this gig, then I'mma break ties with you all together. Lastly, when I feel like you're doing well enough you gon' chip in on some of these bills. Is that understood?"

He nodded, and I blessed him into the game.

Chapter 12

Blaze wanted to fly me out to Milwaukee, Wisconsin because she was doing a major show out there at one of their many strip clubs. She said that she'd put me up at the Hyatt, which was a high-priced hotel that catered to celebrities.

"Baby, all I want you to do is come up here and fuck the shit out of me for a full night. I'll pay for your plane ticket, and I'll make sure that you leave with some real money. Can you do that for me?"

Later that night I was at the airport. I caught a direct flight to Mitchell International. The airport was in downtown Milwaukee. As soon as I walked out of the door she ran to me and jumped in my arms, wrapping her legs around me, kissing all over my lips like she hadn't seen me in years.

We rolled away in a stretch Navigator limo. It was all pink inside and had bottles of champagne on buckets of ice. She didn't waste no time attacking me. As soon as I got all the way into the limo she pulled up the partition, and unbuckled my belt, pulling it down far enough to get my dick out.

"I been feigning for this dick, baby. I miss the taste of it." She pulled the skin downward and sucked the head into her mouth, rolling her tongue around the head. I inhaled, and damn near bit a plug through my bottom lip. When her lips got to sucking up and down, I felt my eyes rollin' into the back of my head. She was doing her thing. She popped it out of her mouth.

"When we get in this room I want you to fuck the shit out of me. I want my pussy beat, and I want this dick in my big ass booty. I want you to fuck me just like a slut."

I grabbed a hand full of her hair roughly and pulled her head back. "Bitch, don't tell me what to do. This my muthafuckin' pussy. I got this shit!"

I pushed her off of me and threw her on to her back. I hit the switch and pulled the partition down. "Hey driver, you wanna see this fine bitch pussy?"

I felt the limo swerve as if he'd damn wear hit something. I saw his eyes in the rearview mirror. He was black and older, maybe in his late fifties.

"Oh sir, no I can't get engaged in things like that." I could see that he was nervous, and the look on his face said that he wanted to see Blaze's pussy as bad as I did the first day I saw her. I made her sit on the seat, and I knelt down between her legs and pushed her Gucci skirt over hips, then pulled her panties off of her ankles. She moaned and opened her legs wide.

"Why are you doing me like this, Taurus?" she asked, with a devilish grin, seductively licking her lips.

I moved to the side, reached and spread her fat pussy lips. "Look at this pussy, sir. Look at how fat it is. I bet you ain't seen nothing this fat in a long time, huh?"

The driver stopped at a red light and turned all the way around in his seat. His eyes were wide open. He had them pinned on Blaze's twat, and the longer he looked the wetter she became.

She dug her nails into my shoulder. "He not supposed to be looking at me like that. He's my driver, and he's my father's best friend. It's not right."

I slid two fingers into her and took them deep. She raised off of the seat and moaned into the air. Her pussy was dripping wet and I could smell its essence. The scent was driving me crazy. I ran my fingers in her at full speed and stopped to suck on her clitoris. She screamed and bucked into the air, coming all over my mouth. "That's my father's best friend. He knew me since I was two, oh shit this ain't right!"

The driver pulled the limo to the side of the road. I yanked Blaze out the seat and put her on the floor. Then I laid down and made her straddle me wit her ass facing him. When that hot pussy slid down my dick, I wanted to holler to the moon. It was so wet that I slipped right in. I held her ass open while she rode me like a maniac.

"Ride that dick, baby. Show off for your daddy friend. Show him that you're grown now, and that you get it in."

She pulled her own dress all the way off and exposed her titties to him. Both nipples were erect and juicy. I saw him reach over and massage first one titty, and then the other.

"It's okay, Gerald, you can play wit my titties. I know you been wanting to see them."

She rode me harder while I gripped that big ass booty. She turned and faced Gerald while she bounced up and down on my dick. "Touch me, Gerald, please!"

He pulled on her nipples as he grabbed her head and they started making out. I was hitting her from the back so hard that my abs were hurting. I think seeing that taboo shit between them was driving me crazy.

Before it was all said and done, she gave him some head, and let him play in her pussy. She didn't let him fuck. I didn't have a clue as to why because I was definitely cool with it.

I found out later on that he was indeed her father's best friend. And her best friend was also Gerald's daughter. They had known each other since she was two and she'd always looked at him as a father figure.

When we got to the hotel that night I fucked Blaze in every hole on her body. I mean I treated her like a straight slut and took all of my frustrations out on her pussy. It got so bad that she was crying and still begging me to fuck her harder. That shit turned me on so much. We didn't stop until about three in the morning and by that time, she was crying and breathing heavy at the same time.

"I love the shit out of you, Taurus. Please let me do something for you. I'm begging you." She rubbed my abs and kissed my chest.

I didn't know how I wanted to use her yet, or if I wanted to use her at all. Being honest, I loved the sex just as much as she did. She had some good ass pussy. It was nice and snug. Not too tight that it hurt. I didn't like all that shit. I had a nice sized dick, so I needed for my pussy to have a few miles on it. When I'd fucked Shakia for the first time I enjoyed it, but her pussy was way too tight. I felt like my shit was being smothered. Those niggas that liked super tight ass pussies just had l'il dicks, or they were lowkey pedophiles. At least that's how I felt.

"Baby, what are you doing with your life? Do you have any goals that I can help you with? Can I pay for something for you?"

That question caught me off guard. I had never had a female come at me in that way. It scared me, because it was like she was smacking me in the face with reality. The dope game was not my reality. It was only a short-term dream. "I don't know, baby. All I do know is that I don't want to be in the streets forever. I eventually wanna own my own businesses."

She kissed my chest and licked a nipple. "What kind of business, baby?"

"I'm thinking a barbershop and a few restaurants that my mother and sister could run. I also wanna get into real estate on some level."

She sat all the way up in the bed and tossed her long hair over her shoulders. The room had a strong aroma of sex. The good sex that you had to work. I sniffed the air and smiled. I had definitely worked hard.

"I'm taking real estate classes right now at the University of Texas. I'm also studying Urban Development. Maybe you should enroll into college and get a few degrees. Then when you're ready to start buying property I'll buy you your first apartment complex." She reached over and grabbed the phone. "Are you hungry?"

Replaying everything she had said, I was trying to wrap my head around the fact that she'd offered to buy me an apartment building. But I also was very hungry and I told her that.

We made it through about half of our steaks before we passed out. I mean I fell asleep in mid chew. I was so tired that I could barely hold my fork right, and she was the same.

The next day we didn't leave the room until the afternoon. She insisted that we spend a day out on the town, so we drove a few hours away from Milwaukee and hit up a place called Noah's Ark. It was a large water park that had rides and everything. We ran around that place like little kids chasing one another. I really wasn't the swimming type, and luckily this place wasn't like that. It was filled with roller-coaster water rides, and we got on damn near every one of them.

After we left there we went and played laser tag. They had this little jungle like place inside of a darkened dome, and we had our own laser guns. We went on missions and zapped the other couples that were there. I had never had that much fun, even as a child. The cards life had dealt to me forced me to grow up before it was my time.

That night we went to a five-star restaurant named Emilio's. It was located in the heart of Milwaukee. Our car was valet parked, and we were escorted to our table by a waiter that had a white cloth over his forearm. He was dressed in a nice tux. I was very impressed. We were seated in a dimly lit corner of the room where less than twenty feet away a band played on stage, and a short man sang a melody that was previously sung by Frank Sinatra. It was nice and elegant. Immediately, I could tell that Blaze had been raised with many experiences and opportunities than I had had the pleasure of experiencing myself.

Blaze took my hand, interlocking her fingers into my own. "This is living right here, Taurus." She leaned her head on my shoulder, and I could smell her perfume. She smelled so good. I loved it.

"This is the kind of life that I want to live. I like to think outside of the ghetto, because I know my family deserve better than that."

She nestled her face into my neck. "You're always talking about your family. What about you? What do you in particular want out of life?"

I didn't know how to answer that question, because when I thought about life the first person I thought about was my mother, then my little sister. I didn't know what I needed or wanted specifically, because everything I did I did it for them first and foremost. I shrugged my shoulders.

"I don't know." Blaze functioned on a totally different level. She was always saying stuff to make me think. Honestly, I didn't have a clue what I ultimately wanted to do or what types of experiences I wanted to have, because I've been in survival mode all this time. It's hard to have the luxury of dreaming when you're just trying to make it through another day.

She kissed my neck. "Well, whenever you figure it out, I'm going to make sure you're able to obtain it, I promise."

Chapter 13

Before me and Blaze decided to call an end to our meeting, she took me to the dealership and bought me a brand-new Range Rover Sport. Black on black with the all-white leather interior. You should have seen my face when I was driving off of the lot. I looked like a kid leaving a candy store with a big ass bag of goodies. I really didn't know how to act, or how to thank her because I had not asked her for nothing. She'd took it upon herself and snatched it up for me. Before I left she told me that she would be in touch.

I drove that bad boy all the way back to Memphis. I loved how smooth it coasted on the highway. I got to bumping some of that good Yo Gotti, and before you knew I was pulling into Memphis with my head nodding.

When I got there, it was storming real bad. I pulled up in front of my mother's house, just as Juice was pulling up. I made my way out of the truck, and before I could make it into the house Juice ran on the porch and pulled my arm. I jerked it away from him, and frowned.

"What's good, nigga?" I asked, looking him up and down. His eyes were bucked. He looked like he was wide awake and wired.

He wiped the rain off of his face. "Bro, I need you to ride with me. I don't trust nobody but you, and right now I just need for you to be my brother." He jogged back into the rain and opened his car door. I could see the interior light come on. He threw his arms into the air. "Let's go!"

Something told me right then to go into the house and leave him alone. I had one of those feelings that I was about to get caught up in some bullshit. But I decided against my better judgment. I jogged to his car and got in, taking a glance over my shoulder once to look at our house. As soon as I got in the car he stepped on the gas.

We rolled in silence for about two minutes when he lit a cigarette. "I fucked up, Taurus. I fucked up so bad man I don't know what to do," he said, taking a strong pull from the cigarette and inhaling.

I felt chills go down my spine. I didn't know what it was, but for Juice to be admitting that he messed up, it had to be something huge. I pulled my seatbelt across my chest, because he was driving erratic.

"Bro, first of all you need to chill. Secondly, tell me what I'm about to walk into."

"That nigga, Pac man, got me in some bullshit and I gotta make things right before it's too late." He rolled down his window and flicked the cigarette butt out of it. He turned the corner so hard that I wound up against the passenger door. It looked like he was about to crash into the stop sign at the end of the street, but luckily, he missed it by inches.

My heart was beating so hard in my chest. I felt like I could barely breathe. I didn't like the fact that he was being so vague. The only time he got like that was when he had done something serious.

He grabbed a bottle of Sprite that had turned pink from the Lean he'd added to it, and took big gulps from it. "I gotta handle my business. That's the only way all of this shit is going to work out. I fucked up by trusting him, but now I gotta handle my business," he said more to himself than me.

When we got on to the highway, I started to panic. "Bro, where are we going?" He stepped on the gas, and turned up the Twista CD. Adrenalin rush bumped through the speakers. I wanted to turn his radio down, but instead I sat back in my seat and got on my phone. I saw that Blaze posted some of our pictures to Facebook and all over Instagram. She left me a message that said she loved me, and that our next trip was going to be Cali. I hit her back and told her I was all for it.

When Juice got off on a country backroad, drove for a little while before pulling up to a farmhouse, I got paranoid as fuck. I got to hearing my father's voice in my head when he said that one of us was going to kill the other one. I thought that Juice had finally lost his mind and that he was bringing me out to the country to splash me.

He turned his whip off, got out, and slammed the door. "Follow me." He jogged toward the barn and I followed him, reluctantly.

Whoever owned the farm had not mowed the lawn in a long time. The grass came up to my waist. With the rain coming down like it was, it made it icky and real slippery. Me and Juice nearly fell twice, before we got up to the red barn that needed to be repainted. He opened the big door and I followed him inside. He allowed for me to walk past him, before closing the door behind me.

The barn had hay all over the place. There was a big chicken coop, where about thirty chickens were. It was a rather large barn, and for the most part empty. Juice pointed to a corner where I could see a light shining from a distance. I walked in that direction.

"Juice, what the fuck are we doing here, man?" It didn't feel right. I was conscious of him walking behind me. You know that feeling you get when you feel like you're about to get hit with something, where you're basically preparing for the assault? Well, that's the feeling that I had with him walking behind me, but I felt like I was about to be shot. I don't know why I thought like, but I did. I kept hearing our father's voice in my head.

As soon as we made it to the corner of the barn I saw Pac Man standing over a white girl who was tied to a chair. She looked like she had been beaten badly. In the hay before them was a white dude. He laid on his back, on his chest I could see that he had four big holes in it.

Juice snapped, "What the fuck you do?" He looked down at the man. He dropped to his knees and put two fingers to the man's neck, checking for a pulse, I assumed.

I could not believe what I was seeing. I got sick to my stomach immediately. Not only was there a dead white dude in my presence, but the white girl they had tied to the chair was naked, and looked to be bleeding from between her legs. I was ready to pass out.

"Dude bitch ass didn't wanna cooperate, so I had to make an example out of his ass. Now this bitch better tell us where this dope at, or I'm killing her next. Word is bond!" He put the .9 millimeter to her forehead and I could hear her squeal through the gag in her mouth.

"Fuck! Nigga, I told you we wasn't killing nobody. Now you done killed a whole ass white dude. They about to cook our black asses," Juice said, running his hands over his face. "Fuck!"

Pac Man waved him off. "I don't give a fuck about no Cracker. Fuck them, and like I said when I take this gag back out of this bitch's mouth, and she don't tell us what we need to hear, I'm smoking her, too. "He grabbed the woman by the throat, and pulled her gag out of her mouth. "Where is the dope, bitch?"

"Now keep in mind what I just said. If you don't tell me what I need to hear I'm smoking yo ass, A-sap!"

"No, you don't have to do that. There in the house, downstairs, in the basement. Just move the washing machine away from the wall, and you'll see a small trap door. All you have to do is kick it in and you'll see all of the dope wrapped in tin foil. Upstairs in my grandmother's room you'll find $100,000 under the floor in her closet. Look in the section of blue dresses, directly downward, you'll find a latch, just pull it up, and the money will be in an old suitcase. There is also jewelry." Tears were pouring down her face. I could hear the trembling of fear in her voice as she spoke, her whole body shook in fright, not knowing what he'd do to her.

Pac Man smacked her so hard that she fell out of the chair, after screaming out loud. "That's for playing with me in the first place."

She landed on her side with her face in the way. "But I didn't. Please don't kill me. I've told you everything that you need to know. I swear I won't tell anybody about this."

Juice pushed Pac Man in the back. "Let's go see if she telling the truth about everything, then we'll decide what we'll do with her later." He pulled out a .45 automatic. "You stay with her l'il bro, and make sure she don't do no shit stupid. We'll be right back."

I nodded, and they left out of the barn, closing the big door behind them. As soon as they did I helped the woman to sit upright in her chair. It just didn't look right to me wither all leaned over like that. I knew that this was in the name of business, but I wasn't going to take the violent approach with no female hostage. That just seemed pussy to me.

I got her to sit upright and was about to put her gag back in place when she started to cry.

"Please don't do this. Please don't let them kill me. I'm begging you. I come from a good family. We've never hurt anybody like this. I've given them everything that I possibly could, so there is no reason to hurt me any further."

I could smell the blood between her legs. That mixed with the scent of the dead dude was getting the best of me. I wondered if she was hurt somewhere in her vagina, so I asked her that question.

"No, I'm not. That guy raped me before you guys got here, and I'm on my period. He didn't even care. So, the blood you see is from that."

Now I was sick to my stomach. One thing I hated was a rapist. I never liked that nigga Pac Man to begin with. But imagining him raping a female while she was tied up really made me hate the nigga guts. I was all for hitting a lick, but I would never rape one of the victims.

"Yo, who is this dude he killed?"

She burst out into tears. "He was my little brother, and he haven't been in the States for a full six months yet. They were supposed to do a deal, but it went south pretty fast." Snot ran down her nose. "He was my everything. I don't know what I'm going to do without him."

My mind got to racing. Juice had me in the middle of some bullshit. This was murder, rape, kidnapping, home invasion, and a list of other things. Not only that, but we were in the racist state of Tennessee. I couldn't do nothing but shake my head. I looked down at the dead man and said a silent prayer for him in my head.

"If you let me go I'll get you a million dollars." She bugged her eyes out of her head. "Listen to me, because I'm not kidding. My family is filthy rich. We have money all over the world. I'll get you a million dollars in less than a week. I swear it."

Just as she said this Juice and Pac Man opened the door to the barn, coming in with duffel bags. "Bro, we about to be out. Everything she said was in there was. Now it's time to get out of this hick ass town."

Pac Man walked up on the woman and cocked his gun. "Say your prayers bitch!"

I pushed him aside and stood in front of her. He and Juice gave me a look that said I had lost my mind. "Before you do that you need to hear her out."

Pac Man mugged me and frowned. "I don't care what this bitch gotta say."

"I'll give you guys a million dollars apiece. I swear to it. I know my life is worth at least that to my family, and that's peanuts. We make that amount in one business deal in an hour, daily."

Pac Man got ready to blow her brains out again, when this time Juice grabbed him. "Wait a minute, nigga, damn. This bitch just said a million apiece. Let's hear her out." He knelt down in front of her. Say, what's your name anyway, baby?"

"It's Nastia." Tears ran down her cheeks.

"And say we was to believe you, how would you make this happen?"

"I'd get in touch with my father, and he'd have you the money right away. He loves me. I'm his only daughter. He has six sons, well, five now because..." She broke into a fit of tears. "Please don't kill me. The money is as good as yours. We'll wire it anywhere, just please trust me."

"Man, fuck this bitch, bro. This would be the dumbest shit we ever did. Matter of fact..." He took his pistol, and raised it up to point at her head when there was a loud ear shattering *Boom! Boom! Boom!* Brains splattered all over my face and neck. I felt the hot blood on my cheeks, and for a brief second, I was in shock.

Pac Man fell onto the dead man that he'd killed. Juice stood over him and shot him three more times in the face.

"I'm tired of you thinking you running the show. I done told you about that too many times already," he said as Nastia screamed at the top of· her lungs. "Bitch, shut up before the next bullets go into you."

I took my shirt and wiped my face. Looking down at Pac Man, I saw the way his head opened with the brain matter all over it, and I felt nothing. The only thing that kept going through my mind was that he was a rapist, and he got what he deserved.

"Now tell me what you were saying, and you better make it make sense."

She broke down every portion to myself and Juice until he decided that he was going to take her up on her offer. I really didn't want no parts of it, but I guessed I was in too deep.

That night we buried Pac Man and the white dude in the corn field about three miles down. It took us nearly four hours to dig those graves and to bury them. By the time we were finished I was drenched in sweat and exhausted. Juice took Nastia to one of he and the Bloodz's abandoned buildings. I didn't follow him and I didn't ask anything more about her or the situation. He gave me three kilos of heroin, and twenty thousand dollars. I was cool with that.

Chapter 14

It blew my mind when Juice showed up at the house two days later with his arm wrapped around Pac Man's sister. Her name was Princess. She was 5 feet 4 inches tall, and about 116 pounds. She had caramel skin, and short curly hair. Her lips were thick and juicy, and although she was slim, she had the nicest round ass that I have ever seen on a slim female.

Before Juice killed Pac Man, he had already sent for his sister to move to Memphis. She'd been going through some painful things with her family that at that time I didn't know too much about. All I knew is that her mother had almost killed her, and that she had to get out of New Jersey before something crazy happened. I didn't know what that meant entirely, and I didn't feel like it was my business to find out.

Juice introduced her as his woman. He was like, "L'il bro, this Princess right here, Pac Man's sister. This my baby, and who I'm gon' wind up wifing." He wrapped his arms around her and rubbed her booty. "Gone give my brother a hug, baby." He demanded pushing her in my direction.

I was outside washing my truck with my shirt off. I had minor specks of soap suds all over me, but that didn't stop her from coming up to me and looking me in the eyes. Hers were Asian-like, and a golden brown. I had to admit that she was beautiful. I was feeling her l'il small self. I pulled her into my embrace and she molded to my body. She felt so good in my arms all small and petite like that. Before her, I had never seen a really slim black woman before that I found attractive. It wasn't because I wasn't into slim women, because I loved all sized women, but I had never took the time out to really appreciate the beauty of a slim chick before, but right then I really was. I squeezed her a little tighter than I had meant to and she moaned a little in my ear. I held her for a minute, and reluctantly let her go. She took a step back and smiled. Looking me up and down before running her hand over my abs. "Damn, what you work out every day or something?"

I ain't gone even lie, I was tightening my stomach on purpose. I had to stunt real fast. She had me feeling some type of way, and I wanted to play into that.

"Where you from, Princess?"

She kept her eyes on my stomach, and bit into her lower lip. "I'm from New Jersey, but I was born and raised in Haiti." She rubbed my stomach again. "Juice, you gone have to step yo game up, because I want you to have abs like these. I think I deserve that." She walked backward looking me in the eyes before bumping into him.

Juice had physically let himself go. He still had a nice muscle mass, but now he had a gut. He didn't work out anymore, and that dope had gotten the best of him for the most part.

"Fuck some abs. That's what I got all of this dick for, so I ain't gotta work out." He took a cigarette from behind his ear and lit it. "L'il bro, I'm expecting that paper to touch down from that move real soon, so stay close."

Princess turned around and kissed his lips. "Where is my brother at? I thought you said he was supposed to have been back early this morning?" she asked him.

"I told you that nigga on the run, so ain't no telling. He ain't got up wit me in a few days, so I don't know." He looked over her shoulder directly into my eyes. "What I saw scared me, because all I saw was ice. My brother was coldhearted. He gave me a look that said he didn't give a fuck and that I had better keep his secret. I curled my lip at him and continued washing my truck.

"Yeah, I heard you, bro, just hit me up when you need me."

Shakia came out of her house with her mother close behind. Juice let go of Princess, and damn wear broke his neck to get to her. As soon as he reached her he pulled her into his arms, and hugged her with his eyes closed. Took a step back and kissed her on the forehead.

Shakia hugged him back, and I noted that her eyes were closed as well. After he kissed her on the forehead I saw his hand go under her shirt rubbing her belly. She laughed and they acted like I wasn't even there.

Shaneeta walked over to me shaking her head, before wrapping her arms around my neck, and kissing me on the cheek. "How are you doing, baby?"

It took all the willpower I had inside of me to not grab her ass in front of her daughter. I wanted to flex on Shakia so bad right there. Especially when I heard her and my brother talking about the pregnancy, and her showing him the ultrasound pictures. I had been wit her to every doctor's appointment, and anytime she needed anything I broke my neck to make sure she got it, and that included money. I made sure I hit her hand every single day. She was still on the whole us being together thing, and I wasn't. The more she pressured me to be with her the more I was thinking about Blaze, and the freedom that came along with being with her.

I ran my hands over her hips, and stopped them at the small of her back. Whispering in her ear, "You know if your daughter keep playing wit me I'm gon' be over there to fuck you in this fat ass booty. It's been calling me anyway." I put my lips real close to her ear so that they were touching it. "You still got the best pussy I ever had."

She smiled then hit me on the chest playfully. "Boy, you betta stop that before you get both of us in trouble. She can hear you."

I turned around to see Shakia staring down the street like she was looking for somebody. I knew that she was just trying to ignore me and her mother. I found that to be funny as hell, and a little immature. "I'm just tired of playing games. I ain't got time for that."

She smiled warmly. "Y'all gone be okay. She just want you all to herself like I do. You can't blame a girl for that." She kissed me on the cheek again. "Come get your plate tonight, too, I'm cooking your favorite."

I lowkey slipped her a few hundred dollars, and she winked at me. I walked up to Shakia, just as she was getting in her mother's car. "Let me holler at you for a minute."

She rolled her eyes. "What you gotta holler at me about all of the sudden?"

I didn't feel like getting into no childish disputes with her. I moved her out of my way a little, and stuck my hand in the car. "Shaneeta let me roll yo car around block real fast, while I holla at her. I'll be right back"

She nodded and told me to hurry back. As soon as we peeled away from the curb, Shakia released a river of tears.

What the fuck is wrong with you and my mother? Why y'all gotta do that shit in front of me like that? she whimpered, through sniffles.

I exhaled. "You ain't got no room to talk. You got my brother all under your shirt rubbing on your stomach and shit like that's cool. What's got into you?" I asked, giving her a look of disgust.

"Me? What's gotten into you? It's like we don't have no kind of relationship no more. Our whole relationship revolves around doctor's appointments and you giving me this guilt money."

"Guilt money, what's that?" I asked parking the car and turning off the ignition.

She wiped her tears away from her cheeks. "That's the money you give to me to pacify me. You know that you're supposed to be doing the standup thing, which is being with me, but you're not, and your only way of making yourself feel better is to give me money. I guess you think that can fill in the blanks of your actual physical presence."

I exhaled loudly. "I don't want to get into all of that, Shakia. I just need to know if you need anything, or if there are any bills I can pay for you or your mom? Are you ready for a car? Is there anything that I can do for you?"

She shook her head. "Nope, not for me. As far as bills go I'm sure my mother will tell you all about that when you pick up your plate tonight." She made air quotes with her fingers.

"It's like the harder I try to be there for you the more you create this drama. Why would I want to be in a relationship with you when all we do is fight?" I couldn't understand her logic for the life of me. Ever since she'd found out she was pregnant, all we did was argue and bicker. It got to the point that when I saw her my mood would instantly go down. I didn't like that aspect of things, because before we got involved we were the best of friends. "Is there any way we could ever go back to being just friends??

She cracked her window. "I don't even know who you are anymore. You're definitely not the man that I let take my virginity." She broke down crying. "I just can't understand why you don't want to be with me? What is so wrong about me? Why am I not worthy of your loyalty?" She asked grabbing my hand and interlocking her fingers with mine.

I hated when she took me here. It wasn't that I didn't want to be with her, or that there was anything wrong with her that prevented me from committing to just her. I just didn't want to be tied down, it was as simple as that. "Shakia, I love you. I always have and that will never change. I'm just not ready to be in no long-term relationship. I'm only 18. Now I'm going to be there for you for the rest of my life. I promise you that, but you have to allow me to mature into the state of mind that you're pushing, because I'm not there yet, and you can't force me to be. All you're doing is pushing me further away from that state of mind."

She looked out of her window. "You know what, Taurus, I

just thought you were different."

I pulled her hand to my lips and kissed it. "One day." I grabbed her purse and put a G in it. She always made it seem like she ain't want the money, but she was never stubborn enough to give it back.

I drove away from the curb and back around the corner to our house. Juice was still in the front yard with Princess and Shaneeta. He was doing some sort of crazy dance and Shaneeta was cheering him on, while Princess looked like she wanted to be anywhere else but there.

Shakia reached over and squeezed my thigh. "I really love you, Taurus, and one day soon I hope you'll find it in your heart to love me enough to be with me and our child. We deserve to have a better family than what our parents gave us. You're my heart and soul." She kissed me on the cheek then got out of the car.

Princess made her way over. She opened the door to Shaneeta's car and got in. "Damn, I ain't know yo brother was this corny. He make me miss Jersey." She laughed and patted my thigh. "Are you alright? I can tell baby momma drama when I see it. I got a few sisters, so I know what it is."

I nodded my head, even though I ain't know how to feel. Every time I got around Shakia she always put too much on my brain at one time. A part of me wanted to just say forget it and be with her faithfully. But I just knew in my heart that it wouldn't last long. I loved pussy way too much.

"I don't really know how her and your brother get down, but I wasn't feeling all of that affection they were showing each other. That was too much. Are they always like that?"

I shrugged my shoulders. "To be honest that was my first time really peeping some shit like that, and I wasn't cool with it. I just told her ass that when we rolled off. I figured I'd try and be classy about the situation and not make a scene. But on every level, that was inappropriate."

She nodded. "Yeah, I agree."

I watched Shaneeta point at Juice as he was doing some new move. Shakia waved them off and looked as if she were on her way into the house. Something told me to look ahead, and boy am I glad that I did, because riding down the street in an all blue drop top Mustang was about four dudes with blue bandanas over their faces, and assault rifles in their hands.

As soon as I saw them, it was like their car sped up. It came to a halt in front of our house, and before I knew what I was doing, I had shot out of the car, running full speed just as the guns went off sounding like a loud ass typewriter.

Taat, taat, taaat! Boom! Boom! Boom! I got to Shakia and tackled her to the ground, throwing my body on top of hers. *Blocka! Blocka! Blocka!*

I looked to my right and saw Juice shooting back at the car. Shaneeta tried to run, and got hit twice in her back, she did a 180, and fell in the grass. Juice fell to the grass, shooting at their car. He had two guns in his hands, and both were barking. I could hear the windows shattering in Shakia's house. She screamed under me, and I held her more firmly to the ground. It seemed like the gun battle went on for a whole hour, but it couldn't have been more than thirty seconds before they were peeling away from our block with Juice chasing them down the street bussing.

After they left, I got Shakia up and took her into the house. She tried to grab a hold of me.

"I love you so much, Taurus. I love you so fucking much!" I don't think she knew that her mother had been shot. I told her to go into the bedroom and get under the bed. I kissed her on the forehead and once again she tried to grab me.

I ran outside just in time to see Juice carrying Shaneeta to his car. Once she was in, Princess peeled away from the curb, and I followed close behind in my truck, praying that we would make it to the hospital in time. I prayed that she wouldn't die. I prayed that she would be okay. She did not deserve those bullets. Something told me that all of them were meant for Juice. It was crazy how oftentimes the bullets found the innocent. Life didn't make sense.

We waited in the emergency room for three hours straight before a doctor came out and told us that the surgery was a success, and that she would be okay. She was already awake when we got to her room. I was surprised because she even had a smile on her face. That warmed my heart. I walked right over to her bedside and kissed her on the lips, and then the forehead.

"You're a warrior, Shaneeta."

They had her laying somewhat on her side. The gauze on her back were still bleeding.

"I'm not a warrior it's just not my time to go yet." She licked her lips and swallowed.

"Yo, this is fucked up, Aunty. I want you to know that when I find them niggas I'mma kill they ass. I hate that this happened to you, but don't worry because I got this shit." Juice promised kissing her on the forehead.

She swallowed. "Boy, that ain't gone solve nothing. I'm still gone have been shot, and all you're going to do is add to the murder rate of our people."

Juice nodded. "You damn right. Them niggas came over there popping at my people. You think I ain't finna go knock some heads off! I'm fucking over mothers, kids, the whole sha-bang. Ain't nothing off limits after this!" he bellowed, leaning over her.

She shook her head. "You really don't get it do you. These boys know where your mother lay her head. What's to stop them from hurting her or one of your siblings? Do you even think that far into things?"

Juice frowned. "That's why I gotta kill they ass. The less of them that are walking around the better chances I have of my people being safe and sound."

"Juice, get out of my face before I try and get up out of this bed and kick your tail. You're pissing me off right now. Get away from me!" She screamed with tears coming down her cheeks. "Matter fact, get out of my room!"

Juice looked hurt. "Really?" He nodded. "Alright then. Whatever, let's go Princess." He wrapped his arm around her shoulder.

She shook it off and walked to the bed. "I'm sorry that this happened to you. You are an inspiration. If there is anything that I can do for you, please let me know." She kissed her cheek and waved bye to me.

"Taurus, come here, baby," she whimpered, looking at me from the corners of her eyes.

I got to her bedside and slightly sat on it, taking her hand into mine. "I'm so glad that you're okay. You mean a lot to a lot of people, especially me and your daughter."

She tried to swallow and a tear ran down her cheek. "I saw what you did for my daughter back there and I gotta say that you are more of a man than I have ever seen. I am jealous of her because she has you. I know that in time that you will do right by her if you choose to take it there. But, I just need you to know that I am addicted to you, Taurus. I don't think I will ever be able to stay away from you because you do something to me that I can't describe." She cried harder. "I wish that you were mine. I wish that we could continue doing what we do, but I feel like this happened to me for a reason. I know that we are hurting my daughter every time we get down. We can't do that no more. This is Jehovah's way of telling me that."

My head was so cloudy by what had taken place that afternoon that I didn't know how to respond to what she was saying. I was having a hard time thinking straight. One thing was for sure, I didn't want to lose her, and had I been near her when the guns started popping, I would protected her as well. I leaned down and kissed her forehead.

"I got your back, Shaneeta, and I'm gone make sure you're straight when you come out of here. You're not going back to that house. I'm letting you know that right now."

She nodded as more tears fell down her cheeks. There was a knock on the door. I looked to see to black detectives wearing suits. They had a big golden badge that hung on their belt, making them easily identifiable. "Excuse us, but we need to speak with the victim."

I felt chills go up and then down my spine. I kissed Shaneeta again on the lips. "I'm gone be in touch. Shakia gone be on her way down here. If you need me for anything, don't hesitate to reach out to me. You understand that?"

"Yes, now get out of here while I talk to them."

As I was coming out of the hospital, Tywain was pulling up. I saw him and he jumped out of his whip, damn near running me over. "Bro, we gotta get over to my grandparent's house right away, it's urgent."

What else could go wrong? What a day! I thought as I made my way to the truck, heading to put out one more fire.

Chapter 15

As soon as we got there I saw the big black Hummer in the driveway. Tywain got out of his whip behind me, so when I got out of mine I followed him into the house. When we walked in I saw Serge and Russell. They looked like they had been up for days. There was also two other white men there that gave me a weird feeling. They looked at me as if they hated my guts. The scowls on their faces yelled hatred.

Lily appeared from upstairs. She threw her coat on and walked right past me without speaking. I found that incredibly odd. She got into her car outside and I could hear her peeling away from the curb.

Russell walked over and shook my hand. "How you doing, son?" he asked giving me that handshake that always made me want to punch him.

"I'm good. What's going on?" I asked looking around. I could tell that it was something fishy. I just couldn't quite put my finger on it.

Serge moved Russell out of the way and walked up to me. "You have a good grasp of the streets, yes?"

I frowned looking around. "A little. Why? What's good, Serge, man?"

"I am willing to offer you a million dollars if you can help me find the man that kidnapped my son and daughter. Both of them are missing and yesterday I received a message from the kidnapper. He sent my son's three fingers and says that if I don't pay him three million dollars that he's going to kill both of my children. Their grandparents home was burned to the ground by I am guessing by the same bandit."

My eyes bugged out of my head. I started to feel sick on the stomach. "Do you have a picture of them?" I asked, praying that his kids weren't who I thought they were.

He held up his phone, and as soon as I saw the picture of the girl I damn near fainted. I did all I could to not reveal what I knew with my actions. "This is my baby girl, and this is a picture of my youngest son." He flipped through until the picture went back to his daughter. "She is my only baby girl. I will give the world for her, but this man plays games. He says one thing and then another. I don't have the time. I want my kids back!" he yelled and slammed his hand down on a table. "Now do you have your ear to the streets or not?!"

I looked over at Tywain and he looked off. Serge looked from him back to me, and frowned. "Serge, let me hit the pavement and see what I can find out."

He curled his lip. "You do that and you get back to me immediately! I want to know where my kids are. I will have the whole of Russia here in the States if my babies aren't returned to me. These are my kids. Fruit of my loins. I will not be so nice about them."

Russell patted him on the back and turned to me. "Anything you can find out, Taurus, will be helpful for us. All we care about is getting them back safe and sound. Money is no object. So whatever resources you need you let us know and they will be made available to you. You find them and you're a filthy rich man. I can promise you that," he said before hugging me and patting me on the back.

Before me and Tywain left out of his grandparent's home I couldn't help but to notice how the other Russian men were looking at me. They gave me a look that said they knew I was up to something. It made me paranoid. The first thing on my mind was getting to Juice and trying to find out where he had the woman stashed. I needed to let him know that he was making a huge mistake, and treading waters way deeper than what he knew about.

We got into my truck, and I peeled away from the curb in a

hurry with Tywain in my passenger seat.

"Listen, Taurus, don't be mad at me, man. I know all of that was a complete blindside, but I needed you to know how serious all of this is." He took out a Philly's blunt and lit the tip, before inhaling deeply. "That fool, Serge, is super plugged. Dude got major money down here in the United States and up in Russia. He come from a well-organized, crime family that are deep in the game. They even run shit in the political world. I'm talking, buying senators, rigging elections, all types of shit. When I heard his kids got snatched up, I knew it was finna be trouble." He passed the blunt to me and I held it for a second and gave it back without even pulling off of it. "Yo, what's the deal, kid?"

I shook my head. "I ain't feeling that shit right now. I gotta figure this shit out before it's too late." My head was spinning. If Serge was as plugged as Tywain was making him out to be, then we were in trouble.

He took another deep pull and blew the smoke to the roof of the car. "I know that nigga Juice got his kids. We gotta holla at that fool, and speak some sense into him. If he don't let them go, I can promise you that Serge is going to kill your whole family, including the both of us."

I looked over at him and swallowed. I wanted to snap at him for speaking some shit like that into the atmosphere, but if everything he had said about Serge was true then I knew that he was keeping shit real on the other end. I got to thinking about my mother and little sister, and I felt sick. They should never have to suffer over some shit that they had nothing to do with.

Tywain turned up the A.C. in my truck. "Do you know where he at right now?"

I shook my head. "Nall, but go in your phone and see if that nigga on Facebook right now." I was on my way to our house. I wanted to get my sister and mother out of the city until all of this blew over. I would never be able to sleep at night if anything happened to them on account of what me and my brothers did in the streets.

"Yeah, that fool on there. You want me to tell him anything in specific?"

"Tell bro to meet me at our mother's house right now. That it's an emergency." I sped the car up a little bit as I entered the highway.

Twenty minutes later I pulled up in front of my mother's house just as her, my brother Gotto, and my sister were unloading grocery bags. Gotto tried to pull me aside as I got out of my truck. He literally met me in the street. I sidestepped him and told him that I would holler at him in a minute. I walked right up to my mother and hugged her, kissing her on the cheek.

"I need you to listen to me, momma."

She took a step back out of my embrace and looked me up and down. "What's the matter, baby? You're scaring me."

I grabbed the grocery bag out of her hand. "Look, I want you to take my truck and drive over to New Orleans, and stay with Aunty Danyelle for a few weeks until I figure some things out back here. I need you to take Mary along with you. "

"New Orleans, boy, are you crazy? I don't want to live in that janky ass city. And why am I leaving Memphis?" She grabbed another bag out of the back of her car. I took that one out of her hands as well.

"Because it's not safe here. Now get in my truck and get out of here. I'm not playing right now." I gave her a look that told her I was dead serious.

Her eyes got bucked then she smiled warmly. "Okay baby, but how are we supposed to survive? I got about a thousand dollars to my name until I get paid."

"Don't worry about that. You'll have about $50,000 when you hit the road. I'll be right back, but get in my truck, now!" I demanded.

She grabbed my sister's arm and said something to her. I saw them open the doors to my truck and get in. I ran into the house and straight to my bedroom where I dug my stash out of the mattress. I grabbed out five $10,000 rolls, and threw them into a purple Crown Royal bag. I jogged back outside just as Juice was pulling up with Princess in the passenger's seat. I nodded at him, and leaned my head into my truck after giving my mother the keys, and the bag of money.

"Look, momma, if you ain't going to New Orleans with Danyelle, then I'mma need you to go up to St. Louis with Aunty Amanda, until I either send for you or come up there to get y'all."

"What's going on, Taurus? Do this have anything to do with Shaneeta getting shot? "My sister asked with tears in her eyes.

I took a deep breath. I hated when she cried, or any woman for that matter. But this was my baby sister. Her tears hurt my soul. "There is a lot going on right now, and it isn't safe for you women to be here right now."

"But what about you?" she asked now crying harder.

"Yeah, why don't you get in the truck with us, Taurus, right now. Why do you have to stay here? Don't you know that I need you, baby?" my mother said, starting to break down along with my sister. That had me misty eyed. Damn, I hated the effect they had on my emotions.

"I'll be following y'all real soon. I gotta take care of this business first, then I'm gone be out there I promise."

My little sister opened her door and ran around the side of the truck directly into my arms. "I love you so much, Taurus. You're the best big brother in the world. Please come to us real soon."

"I will, l'il momma, I promise." I leaned into the window and my mother kissed me on the lips, before rubbing the side of my face with her fingertips. "I'm your, baby. Remember you told me that, so now I want you, son. Please make it up to me. I deserve your love. I need it." Tears dropped from her cheeks on to her lap.

I nodded my head. "I know, momma, and I promise I'll be up there in a few weeks, if not sooner. I need you just as much as you need me." I wiped her tears away and kissed her on the forehead. "You're my baby. I mean that."

Just as she started the truck, Juice walked up to her window, looking inside and then up to me. "Why she driving your truck?" He looked down at her. "Momma, where you and Mary finna go?"

She looked at him for a full second before frowning. She put the truck in drive and pulled away from the curb. Juice jumped back to avoid her running over his foot. We watched her get to the end of the block and turn right.

"What the fuck wrong wit her?" he asked looking hurt.

I shrugged my shoulders. "I don't know, but I need to holler at you ASAP!"

He looked me up and down. "About what?"

"Let's go into the crib, because this shit is serious," I said already walking in that direction. I got halfway to the porch when I turned around and noticed he wasn't following me. He had his arm around Princess. "Yo. Juice, come on man!" I yelled irritated.

He waved me off. "Nall, I don't feel like talking right now. I gotta take care of this business." He pointed at his car and Princess started walking toward it.

I felt my temper rise and I almost called the nigga out of his name, but I caught myself. "Bro, bring yo ass up here and holler at me. I got some business for you," I said as calmly as I possibly could.

He gave me a look that said he was slightly offended, before following me into the house. "Nigga, what you about to tell me better be very important or we're about to tear this whole house up. I don't like how you just clowned me back there. I should whoop yo ass." He balled up his fist and bit into his bottom lip.

"Yeah, well fuck all that. What's up with that white girl you got ducked off?"

He walked to the living room table and sat down, pulling out a Visine bottle of heroin. I watched as he snorted a few drips up each nostril. "Why you wanna know all that? How you know I ain't bodied her ass yet?"

I sat down across from him and looked him straight in the eyes. "Because you're still alive."

He lowered his eyes. "Oh really?"

"Yo, we gotta cash her in right now while the getting is good. If you keep holding on to her that's gone cause problems for our whole family, and we're already warring with enough niggas in this city. That's why I sent mom and Mary out of town until this whole thing blows over. "

Juice leaned back in his chair, and wiped his mouth with his hand. His eyes were low, and he looked like he was about to fall asleep. "Yo, I got this, l'il brother. You just panicking right now, that's all."

I slammed my hand down on the table. "Fuck that! I'm not panicking! That white girl father is plugged. It's only gone be a matter of time before they find her, and then what you gone do?"

He tried to stand up, but his knees got wobbly. He sat back down and smiled. "Damn, that's some good ass dope." He waved me off. "She been in our basement for three days now and don't nobody even know she down there." He nodded out.

I slapped the table and that woke him back up.

"You see I got all of this under control. I'm gone keep her for a few more days and then I'm gone cash her in. I'm trying to get a few million dollars. All you gotta do is be cool and I'm gon' cut you in real nice." He nodded out again, this time he started snoring.

I slapped the table so hard this time that my hand went numb for a few seconds. "Wake yo ass up!"

His eyes popped open. "If you hit that table one more time, me and you gone have a problem." He stood up and stretched. "I gotta go handle some business and when I get back me and you can talk some more." He stumbled to the front door, and opened it. "You just gotta trust me, little brother. "He pointed to his temple. "You see me and daddy got the same smarts. You just too dumb to see my plan right now." He shook up the bottle of Visine and snorted a few drips up each nostril before leaving out of the door.

I waited until I heard his car start up before I pulled the curtains back. He said something to Tywain and then he and Princess pulled off down the street. I opened the front door and called Tywain inside.

"So, what's good? Did he tell you where they at?"

I shook my head. "Nall, but I need you to run over and holler at Shakia for me. Just make sure she straight while I take a quick shower. Hit my phone before you come back over, because I'm gone lock the door and shit. That nigga, Juice, tripping. We gone have to find them on our own."

Tywain punched at the air. "Fuck! That nigga so damn stupid! Kid, I'm not fucking wit Serge like that. Dude a body both of our asses and our whole family with no remorse over his kids. Take your shower, bro, and let's find them before he whack my grandparents for no reason at all."

As soon as he left out of the house I locked the door. I felt like I was getting a migraine. I went to the backdoor, and unlocked it. I took the stairs down to the basement where it was pitch black. As soon as I turned the lights on I saw her handcuffed up against the wall. She looked skinnier than the last time I saw her. Somebody had taken a sheet, cut a hole in it, and put it over her head, so that's what she wore for clothes. Her feet were bare and shaking like crazy.

I walked up to her and took the gag out of her mouth. She opened her eyes and looked up at me. "How long do I have to stay here?" she said the words so low that I could barely hear her.

I pulled her black hair out her face. "Nastia, I'm gon' get you out of here, but before I do you and I need to come to an understanding."

She lowered her head. "Anything. Just tell me what you want from me. If it's my body like the other men, go ahead and take it. Just get me out of here, please."

I shook my head. "You mean to tell me that you've been sexually assaulted since the other dude that got killed did it to you?"

She nodded. "Yeah, by the same guy that killed him. He hurt me so bad." I saw the tears pour out of her eyes, and that made my stomach flip.

"I'm sorry that you had to go through that. But that's not what I'm on. I ain't no fucking rapist, and I promise you I ain't got nothing to do with this. The dudes that snatched you and your brother up I'm familiar with. That's why you've seen me twice now, but this ain't my lick."

She raised her right leg and scratched the inside of her left one with her foot. "So, then what do you want from me, and why haven't you let me go?" she whimpered.

"I know your father. I know that he is a very powerful man. Now one of the men that kidnapped you I am related to him and I am afraid that when your father finds out that he's going to kill my entire family. That is beef that we don't need. So, I would like to make a deal with you that you must keep."

"Anything, I will literally do anything you tell me to do. I promise."

I rubbed her small face, and wiped her tears away with my thumbs. "I need for you to not pin my brother for this. I need for you to let him skate, and in turn I will release you and make sure that no one harms you ever again."

She shook her head from right to left. "I promise you on the God above that I will not say anything. If need be I will tell my father that white men did this to me. Just let me go, please."

I nodded. "Okay, all I need is for you to give me an hour. I will be back and when I get back I will release you, and take you to your father myself. We'll tell him that two dope addicts kidnapped you, and demanded money. That when I told them I was putting up a kilo of heroin as bounty for you, one of them folded, and gave me the drop on where you was, and I found you in a basement."

She shook her head. "Don't worry, I'll figure out the story, you just get me out of here."

Chapter 16

"I need for you to get in contact with the police and tell them that Juice was one of the shooters."

Shaneeta tried her best to sit up in her hospital bed. Her eyes were opened so wide that I could see the veins in them.

"You want me to do what?"

I paced back in forth in front of her bed. "Look, I know that sound crazy, but if you don't do it then my whole family is going to be murdered in a matter of days."

She wiped her hand over her face. "Why would Juice going to jail stop that from happening?"

"Juice going to jail for a few weeks would save his own life. The longer he stays out on these streets the more people will be out there hunting for him. Plus, he messing with that heroin real tough, and making a whole lot of stupid decisions. Decisions that's losing a lot of lives."

She sat up further in her bed. "Listen to me, Taurus. You know that I love you with all of my heart. I will do anything for you. I just ain't never turned to no police about nothing. They ain't never did nothing positive for our people." She paused to take a deep breath. "You know they killed my father in front of me when I was just 8 years old?"

I took her hand into my own. "Nall, I ain't know that."

"Yep, they shot him in the head while I sat next to him in our car. I will never forget that day." She blinked tears. "I just hate 'em. But if you're telling me that him being off of the streets will save lives, then I got you. Just tell me what exactly you want me to do?"

Fifteen minutes later I had Juice pick me up. He looked even higher than before. I told him that Shanetta wanted to holler at him at the hospital, and after some intense convincing he finally relented to the idea. Princess was with him. All three of us went up to her room. Me and her sat on the couch while Shaneeta hollered at Juice.

He knelt on the side of her bed, and held her hand. "Holler at me, Aunty."

She turned over to look down on him. "Juice, you know that I love you with all of my heart, but I am worried about you, baby.

"Worried about me, for what?" he asked, looking over to me. "Bro, what you been telling her?"

She grabbed his face. "He ain't told me nothing, I'm making this assumption on my own. I'm worried about you because you're losing yourself. How much of that dope are you doing now?"

He laughed out loud. "Not enough, if you ask me."

She shook her head. "You think everything is a game. What if it were you sitting up here in this bed, or better yet, what if you were in a morgue?"

He shrugged his shoulders. "To be honest with you. I'm sorry that all of this happened to you. And I know it should have been me. But had it been me, I would have rolled with the punches. I don't give a fuck about dying, it gotta happen one day anyway, so why would I give a fuck about when it happen? Ain't nothing on this earth but pain." He switched knees, and continued to hold her hand.

"I'll tell you what, the next time you cuss in front of me, I'm gone pop you in your hardcore mouth. Now you gotta have some respect for somebody, Juice. I'm laying in this bed for you, and you don't even care. Why should I have to send for you to come and see me?" Tears sailed down her cheeks.

Juice kept on swallowing as if he was trying to not allow himself to become choked up. "Yo, I said I was sorry about that. I don't know what else you want me to do?"

Shaneeta rubbed his face. "As handsome as you are, you are

a complete waste to this world. You're so ugly on the inside. That tears me apart."

Juice jumped up. "You know what? I ain't finna keep taking this abuse from you. I said I was sorry. Now that's the best I can do. When you get out of here I'll hit your hand and make sure that you stay cashed out, but for now I'm about to bounce."

As soon as he said that there was a knock on the door, and then it opened. Ten police officers rushed into the room with guns out. Juice looked like he was ready to reach and fire at them. "Deion, put down your weapon, and don't move. We don't want to hurt you."

Juice bit into his bottom lip. "What the fuck y'all want with me?"

The fat police officer in the front who held a shot gun pointed directly at him said, "We just want to take you downtown for some questioning that is all."

"Baby, please just listen to them. I'll be down there to pick you up later on. Just don't do nothing stupid," Princess said standing up.

I was frozen in place on the couch. I didn't know what to say, or to do for that matter. I continued to watch the scene unfold while sweat poured down my back.

Juice looked to Shaneeta. "Bitch, you set me up. I can't believe my own aunty set me up. And my own brother," he said this looking directly at me. "I guess daddy was right. When I get out you better be gone, nigga. That's yo ass." He put his hands up in the air. "Come on Crackas and do ya job."

They rushed him, and tackled him to the floor, before handcuffing him, and leading him away. He gave me the look of death on the way out.

Princess looked me up and down when the police left. "I don't know what just happened here, but I'm gone find out. Until I do I need for you to stay the fuck away from me." She got up and bumped me on her way out of the door.

I kissed Shaneeta on the forehead. "I know that was hard, but I promise I'll explain all of this to you at a later date. I gotta run, and I'll be back later."

I had Tywain pick me up, and take me directly to my house.

"Look, bro, I don't want you to freak out, but his daughter is in my basement right now. That nigga Pac Man already killed his son." Tywain almost hit a parked car. "What the fuck you just say?"

"I said his daughter is in our basement, and Pac Man already killed his son the same day him and Juice snatched them up."

Tywain drove in silence for a long time. "Bro, how long have you known she was in y'all basement?"

"Ever since I told you to go over and check on Shakia while I showered. I took that time to actually holler at her and get an understanding."

Tywain clenched his jaw. "I knew that shit was fishy as hell, because when have you ever locked me out of your house when I came over there?" He shook his head. "Then you hollering this shower shit, and put back on the same ass clothes. That should have told me everything right there."

"Anyway, I wanted to figure some shit out first before I told what was what."

"So, where that nigga Juice at now?"

"Bro just got snatched up by them peoples. He should only be down there for a few weeks though. I knew he was on the run from his P.O., and every time he do that she only keep him for a few weeks."

Tywain took a cigarette and lit it. "What about Pac Man? I usually see him with your brother every day. Now I ain't seen him in a while."

I shrugged my shoulders. "He was about to kill Nastia and Juice bodied his ass."

"What!"

"Yep, shit been real crazy, and now we gotta figure shit out before we drop her off to her old man."

Tywain slammed his hands on the steering wheel. "Nigga, I don't keep shit from you. Yet you done had all of this info, and you been holding it to your chest. I thought we was better than that." He looked hurt.

I ain't know what to say, so I didn't say anything at all until we got to my house. "Why don't you pull around the back, so I can sneak her out the back door? I should be coming out in like five minutes or so."

He nodded his head. "Yeah alright, bro, just hurry up. I still don't know what we finna tell him, but I guess you already got that figured out too." He slumped back in his seat mugging.

I was about to say something to him, but then decided against it. I simply slammed his car door and ran into the house, and had my mind set on going straight into the basement when I bumped into Shakia and Gotto in the living room screwing like crazy. I mean they were right on the carpet in the middle of the floor getting it in. When they heard me come in they scrambled apart. Shakia ran to a corner of the room and started to get dressed.

"I'm so sorry, baby. I'm so sorry. I was vulnerable, and he was holding me and telling me everything was going to be okay."

My brother slipped into his boxers and held his hands up. "Bro, I mean that shit. That's my bad."

I was so caught off guard that I didn't know how to respond. A part of me wanted to snap because they were betraying me. But then again, I really didn't trust neither one of them like that anyway. I got to thinking about him fucking her while my baby was inside of her, and that started to piss me off. But then I got to thinking that what if it wasn't my baby to begin with? I mean who was to say that they hadn't been fucking all along?

After I thought about things for a long time with them watching me closely, I just started smiling. "Congratulations, don't neither one of you muthafuckas mean shit to me no more. Get the fuck out! Both of you. I'm going in the room to get my gun, when I come back out here whoever is present I'm shootin' yo ass dead."

I rushed into my bedroom knowing damn well that I wouldn't have killed neither one of them. I just wanted them out of the house. When I came back out of the room they were both long gone. I had to laugh at that.

I opened the back door and rushed into the basement. There was Nastia, still handcuffed to the wall. I went into the deep freezer and opened the box of fish sticks that my father had way at the bottom of the freezer. That's where he kept the keys to the handcuffs, and they were still there.

As I finished uncuffing her she fell into my arms. "It's okay. I told you I would be back. I have always been a man of my word. Now I need for you to hold up your end, too."

She weakly hugged my neck. "You'll never have to worry about that. I'll keep my promise, especially since your brother didn't kill my brother, but he did kill the man that did. I owe him for that."

I carried her up the stairs and all the way to Tywain's car in the back alley. As soon as I put her in the backseat she started to cry.

I hopped into the passenger's seat, and we sped down the alley on our way to Tywain's grandparent's house.

Chapter 17

"I don't know how you found her so quickly, but what I can tell you is that I am thankful that you brought my daughter back to me. I would still like to know where my son has been buried so that I can give him a proper burial, but his death will not stop me from keeping my promise to you, which we will discuss later on in the week. For now, I would like to spend some time alone with my daughter to get a better understanding of the situation. I will be in touch." Serge shook my hand and looked me in the eye for a long time. "I'll make you rich for this."

I nodded as I felt the butterflies in my stomach. Russell wrapped his arm around my neck, walking me out of his house.

"I don't know how you found her so quickly, but you better hope that it don't come back to you or my grandson, because if it do we will be in hell on earth. However, if y'all are in the clear, prepare to be a rich man."

We were on the porch, and I was ready to get out of there. I had so many things going through my mind that I was getting dizzy. Tywain blew his horn and waved me over to his car. I shook Russell's hand for the last time and was making my way to Tywain's car, when Nastia called my name. She ran out of the house and into my arms.

"Thank you for saving me. I'll keep my promise to you, don't worry. When I'm better, me and you need to have a sit down." She kissed my cheek and walked back on the porch with Russell's arms around her.

I had a hard time going to sleep that night. I had been up for two days straight, so my body was exhausted, yet I could not settle down enough to get into a deep sleep. I laid down at about 2 in the morning, and I didn't drift off until four.

My mind was finally able to rest a little. I didn't get to enjoy it for a long before I was awakened by what felt like a punch to the gut. I woke up coughing. I opened my eyes, and saw that Gotto was holding a sawed-off shotgun in my face.

"Bitch nigga, open yo mouth or I swear on my father's life, I'mma blow yo muthafuckin brains out."

I opened my mouth and he put the barrel of the shotgun into it. Had I not been disoriented and thrown off by just waking up I would have never done that. My brain was barely functioning the way it was supposed to.

"Juice said you got him locked up. He told me to kill you on sight, or he gon' kill me." He looked deranged. I could tell that something was wrong with him. He couldn't have been in his right mind to be doing what he was. He pumped the shotgun and lowered his eyes. "I ain't never felt like you was my brother anyway, die nigga!"

To Be Continued...
Raised as a Goon 2
Coming Soon

Raised as a Goon

Coming Soon from Lock Down Publications/Ca$h Presents

BOW DOWN TO MY GANGSTA

By **Ca$h & Jamaica**

TORN BETWEEN TWO

By **Coffee**

BLOOD OF A BOSS **IV**

By **Askari**

BRIDE OF A HUSTLA **III**

THE FETTI GIRLS **II**

By **Destiny Skai**

WHEN A GOOD GIRL GOES BAD **II**

By **Adrienne**

LOVE & CHASIN' PAPER **II**

By **Qay Crockett**

THE HEART OF A GANGSTA **II**

By **Jerry Jackson**

TO DIE IN VAIN **II**

By **ASAD**

LOYAL TO THE GAME **IV**

By **TJ & Jelissa**

A DOPEBOY'S PRAYER **II**

By **Eddie "Wolf" Lee**

A HUSTLER'S DECEIT **III**

THE BOSS MAN'S DAUGHTERS **III**

BAE BELONGS TO ME **II**

By **Aryanna**

TRUE SAVAGE **II**

By **Chris Green**

RAISED AS A GOON **II**

By **Ghost**

Available Now

(CLICK TO PURCHASE)

RESTRAINING ORDER **I & II**

By **CA$H & Coffee**

LOVE KNOWS NO BOUNDARIES **I II & III**

By **Coffee**

LAY IT DOWN **I & II**

LAST OF A DYING BREED

By **Jamaica**

LOYAL TO THE GAME

LOYAL TO THE GAME II

By **TJ & Jelissa**

PUSH IT TO THE LIMIT

By **Bre' Hayes**

BLOOD OF A BOSS **I II & III**

By **Askari**

THE STREETS BLEED MURDER **I, II & III**

THE HEART OF A GANGSTA

By **Jerry Jackson**

CUM FOR ME

CUM FOR ME 2

CUM FOR ME 3

An **LDP Erotica Collaboration**

BRIDE OF A HUSTLA **I & II**

By **Destiny Skai**

WHEN A GOOD GIRL GOES BAD

By **Adrienne**

A GANGSTER'S REVENGE **I II III & IV**

THE BOSS MAN'S DAUGHTERS

THE BOSS MAN'S DAUGHTERS II

A SAVAGE LOVE **I & II**

BAE BELONGS TO ME

A HUSTLER'S DECEIT I, II

By **Aryanna**

A KINGPIN'S AMBITON

A KINGPIN'S AMBITION **II**

By **Ambitious**

TRUE SAVAGE

By **Chris Green**

A DOPEBOY'S PRAYER

By **Eddie "Wolf" Lee**

WHAT ABOUT US **I & II**

NEVER LOVE AGAIN

THUG ADDICTION

By **Kim Kaye**

THE KING CARTEL **I, II & III**

By **Frank Gresham**

THESE NIGGAS AIN'T LOYAL **I, II & III**

By **Nikki Tee**

GANGSTA SHYT **I II &III**

By **CATO**

THE ULTIMATE BETRAYAL

By **Phoenix**

BOSS'N UP **I & II**

By **Royal Nicole**

I LOVE YOU TO DEATH

By Destiny J

I RIDE FOR MY HITTA

I STILL RIDE FOR MY HITTA

By **Misty Holt**

LOVE & CHASIN' PAPER

By **Qay Crockett**

TO DIE IN VAIN

By **ASAD**

<u>BOOKS BY LDP'S CEO, CA$H</u>
(CLICK TO PURCHASE)
<u>TRUST IN NO MAN</u>
<u>TRUST IN NO MAN 2</u>
<u>TRUST IN NO MAN 3</u>
<u>BONDED BY BLOOD</u>
<u>SHORTY GOT A THUG</u>
<u>THUGS CRY</u>
<u>THUGS CRY 2</u>
<u>THUGS CRY 3</u>
<u>TRUST NO BITCH</u>
<u>TRUST NO BITCH 2</u>
<u>TRUST NO BITCH 3</u>
<u>TIL MY CASKET DROPS</u>
<u>RESTRAINING ORDER</u>
<u>RESTRAINING ORDER 2</u>
<u>IN LOVE WITH A CONVICT</u>

<u>Coming Soon</u>
BONDED BY BLOOD 2
BOW DOWN TO MY GANGSTA

Raised as a Goon

CPSIA information can be obtained
at www.ICGtesting.com
Printed in the USA
JSHW050954110723
44521JS00005B/43